The Uttermares Tales of a Somerset Family

by Sue Delves-Broughton

Best Wishes,
Sue Delves-Broughton.

This book is a work of fiction based on historical fact. The dates on the Uttermare Family Tree and within the text are those found during the author's research. All the key historical events, places and names are real apart from Claire and Ross.

Published by: Fosters
Fosters Farm, Boyshill, Sherborne DT9 5PJ
Printed in the United Kingdom.

For more information contact:
fosters.farm@tiscali.co.uk

Book design: Jo Davies
Cover design: Jo Davies

ISBN - Paperback: 978-1-0369-0414-2

First Edition: November 2024

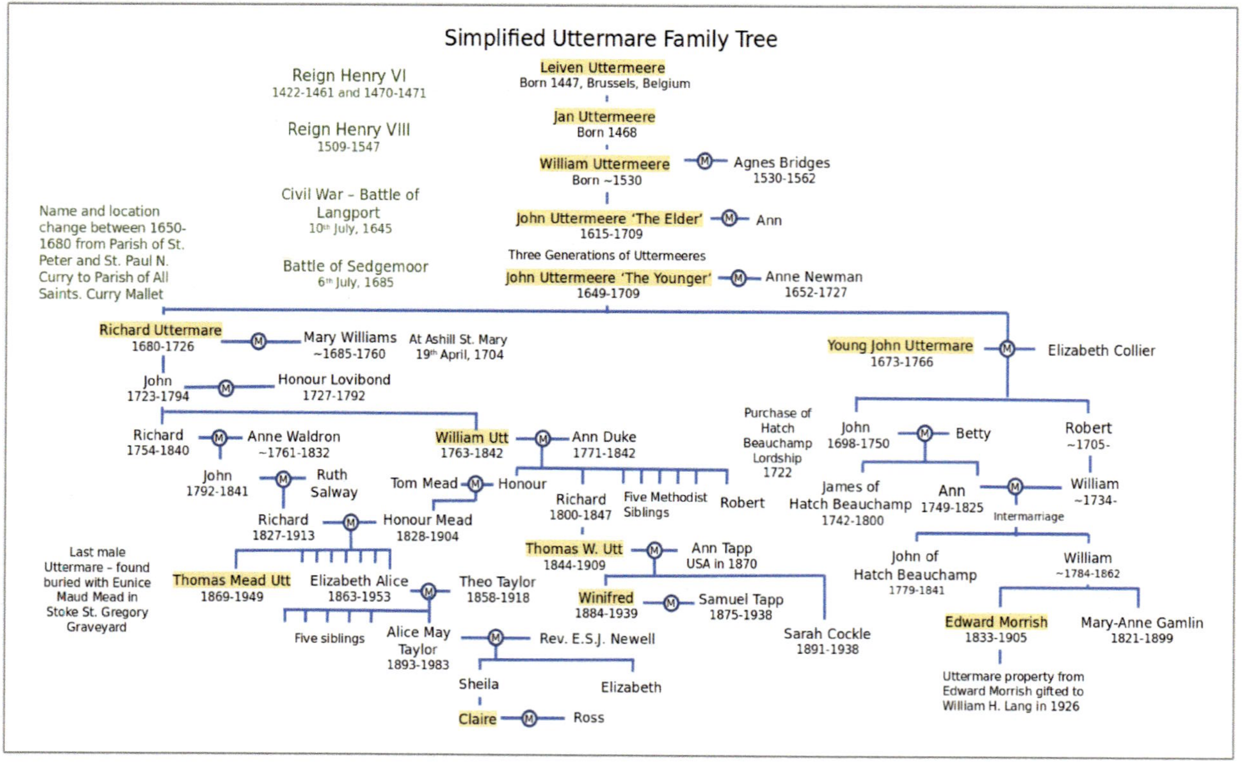
Simplified Uttermare Family Tree
Reign Henry VI
1422-1461 and 1470-1471
Reign Henry VIII
1509-1547
Civil War – Battle of Langport
10th July, 1645
Battle of Sedgemoor
6th July, 1685
Name and location change between 1650-1680 from Parish of St. Peter and St. Paul N. Curry to Parish of All Saints. Curry Mallet
Leiven Uttermeere
Born 1447, Brussels, Belgium
Jan Uttermeere
Born 1468
William Uttermeere
Born ~1530
M
Agnes Bridges
1530-1562
John Uttermeere 'The Elder'
1615-1709
M
Ann
Three Generations of Uttermeeres
John Uttermeere 'The Younger'
1649-1709
M
Anne Newman
1652-1727
Richard Uttermare
1680-1726
M
Mary Williams
~1685-1760
At Ashill St. Mary
19th April, 1704
Young John Uttermare
1673-1766
M
Elizabeth Collier
John
1723-1794
M
Honour Lovibond
1727-1792
Purchase of Hatch Beauchamp Lordship
1722
John
1698-1750
M
Betty
Robert
~1705-
Richard
1754-1840
M
Anne Waldron
~1761-1832
William Utt
1763-1842
M
Ann Duke
1771-1842
John
1792-1841
M
Ruth Salway
Tom Mead
M
Honour
Richard
1800-1847
Five Methodist Siblings
Robert
James of Hatch Beauchamp
1742-1800
Ann
1749-1825
M
William
~1734-
Intermarriage
Richard
1827-1913
M
Honour Mead
1828-1904
Thomas W. Utt
1844-1909
M
Ann Tapp
USA in 1870
John of Hatch Beauchamp
1779-1841
William
~1784-1862
Last male Uttermare - found buried with Eunice Maud Mead in Stoke St. Gregory Graveyard
Thomas Mead Utt
1869-1949
Elizabeth Alice
1863-1953
M
Theo Taylor
1858-1918
Winifred
1884-1939
M
Samuel Tapp
1875-1938
Edward Morrish
1833-1905
Mary-Anne Gamlin
1821-1899
Five siblings
Alice May Taylor
1893-1983
M
Rev. E.S.J. Newell
Sarah Cockle
1891-1938
Sheila
Elizabeth
Claire
M
Ross
Uttermare property from Edward Morrish gifted to William H. Lang in 1926

About the Author

Sue Delves-Broughton lives deep in the Dorset countryside with her husband, two cats and three chickens. She has three grown-up children and six grandchildren. This book is her first novel, based on her experiences whilst tracing her family's history.

Forward

Claire whiles away a snowed-in evening, watching television and dutifully cleaning her Grannie's Victorian, brass milk jug. Under its lid she discovers a note which leads her to ask questions about her family history, and especially about 'The Uttermares'.

The journey leads her down onto the Somerset Levels where she is taken way back to 1447, finding there Leiven Uttermeere, a refugee from Belgium. The name is later to change to Uttermare.

She discovers plaques on church walls, which match up exactly with a stack of ancient family wills that she is unexpectedly given. The names and dates of her family, from late medieval times to the present day, all fall into place like pieces of a jigsaw puzzle.

The Family Tree seems to almost magically create itself. The dates, names and places of the family are all there to be discovered.

Claire feels strangely dissatisfied once she has finished her research - what of the lives of these people? They were real people, some of them living through momentous times.

Once again Claire sets to, researching the history of the Somerset Levels, an area of once marsh and willows but now lush pasture, drained by rhynes and grazed by placid Friesian dairy cows.

She finds that real historical events, like the Civil War Battle of Langport, the Monmouth Rebellion, and John Wesley's visits to the West Country, give life to the real names that she has discovered.

She really didn't have to write the stories of these people's lives. The stories wrote themselves!

Contents

Part 1

Chapter 1 – Discovering the Uttermares

The 'Beast from the East' had arrived. All night long the wind had howled, driving great drifts of snow up against the grey stone walls of the ancient Dorset longhouse. The snow was as high as the hedges in the surrounding fields and the sheep huddled against them, and each other, for protection. Many would not survive.

Claire woke in the morning with the ever-present and immediate thought, 'What have I got to do today?' Claire had recently retired from her work in private practice physio and had always been busy. She missed her work and contact with patients. To compensate, she worked hard in the very large garden surrounding the old, thatched house, rode her horse when the weather was good, shopped, and went to her Zumba class in nearby Sherborne.

She got out of bed and pulled back the curtains to find everything white, with huge snowflakes being driven hard in the wind. This had all been predicted the night before on the News at Ten. 'So, well done the BBC!' she thought.

Later, Claire's husband, Ross, cleared the snow from the back door and made a path over to the stables. At least Mon Amie, Claire's horse, had been snug and safe inside them all night.

There would be no going anywhere for the next three days. All the surrounding lanes were blocked with snow, and the villagers would have to wait for the local farmers, Tom Barton and Jo Hillfield, to come and clear them with their tractors and diggers. However, their own cattle and sheep needed their immediate attention, so it could take a little time.

It was a weird experience just staying in but, unfortunately, one that would become familiar to billions of people the world over very soon. Just like the driving snow that morning, a virus, later to be called Covid 19, would make its way inexorably from the East.

Claire spent the day firstly mucking out Mon Amie, telling her, "Sorry old girl, you've got to stay in like the rest of us!"

Then it was back to the house, generally tidying and cleaning. She imagined that was possibly what many other people might be doing too. Her friend Suzie from a nearby village phoned for a chat. She said she had been emptying, cleaning and sorting out all her cupboards and drawers. That was not Claire's style. She always only did just enough for things in the house to be clean and shipshape.

That evening, Claire and Ross, watched TV. Her somewhat Puritan upbringing dictated that she should not sit idly doing nothing, but that she should, 'Find something constructive to do,' as her mother would have said! So, she decided to clean the collection of brass paraphernalia that sat alongside the wood-burning stove in the huge, old, open fireplace whilst she watched the mid-evening drama. In between the old brass coal scuttle and a second world war shell case holding poker, fire tongs and brush, was a Victorian brass milk jug with a lid. Claire knew this came from her mother's family and that there was a scrap of paper taped inside the lid. She had not properly read it in the past - always being busy with children, horses and life in general.

Now she carefully read it. It was written in her grandmother's beautiful, flowing Edwardian-style script. Her 'Grannie' was Alice May Taylor née Uttermare. It read, *'This milk jug came from Bowdens Farm, Curry Rivel, Somerset, the home of Richard and Honour Uttermare. They had seven daughters and a son Thomas, who was a bachelor. The surname Uttermare has died out.'*

Suddenly, she remembered that a couple of weeks earlier, she had received a long letter from her old school friend, Sandy. Sandy had enthusiastically told Claire how she had recently visited the town of Langport on the Somerset Levels. In the large parish church there, she had found plaques on the walls bearing the names of many Uttermares. She had even copied down the details very accurately and enclosed them in her letter. However, Sandy, never one to mince her words, had added, "You are so lucky. With a name like that, the family tree must be easy to trace," and she ruefully admitted that she had lately been researching her own family name of 'Greenslade' and had not got very far.

All this gave Claire a bit of a guilty feeling. She now asked herself the question, 'Who were these Uttermares who must have been prominent local people and wealthy enough to have their names up on the walls of Langport Church?' Her next question to herself was, 'And why has the name died out?'

Opening her computer, she Googled 'Bowdens Farm'. There it was, a photo of a rather grand, early eighteenth century, Queen Anne style farmhouse in Hambridge, Curry Rivel. It also consisted of a smokery, restaurant, antique shop and a few other outlets. "Hey, I've found it!" she exclaimed to Ross. Peering over her shoulder he said, "I've been there."

"Of course you have!" she replied sarcastically. Ross had been all over the world as a food scientist and it didn't matter where was mentioned, he had been there!

"No," he said. "I have. I visited the smokery about thirty-five years ago when I was involved in eel farming. I know the guy who runs it."

A phone call later to 'the guy', and it was decided that, once the snow had gone, they would go and look for Bowdens Farm.

Copper milk jug with brass banding used for dairy work circa 1850-1899

Wood, M 'The Somerset Levels 1990' oil painting, privately owned

Middleney Farmhouse circa 1860
The photo that Claire found and mistakenly thought was Bowdens Farm.

Chapter 2 – Journeys onto the Levels

The 'Beast from the East' went back from whence it had come, or maybe it continued its journey westward. Spring arrived with snowdrops under the hedges, and hellebores, tulips and daffodils pushing through the blue lias Dorset clay in Claire's beloved flower borders.

Now was the time to visit the Somerset Levels. She and Ross set off in the car on a cold but sunny, blustery day. She had, in her pocket an old sepia photo of a long E-shaped farmhouse, with two women wearing Victorian clothes, and a baby in a carriage-type pram in the driveway. There was some writing on the back of the photo in her Grannie's hand, but it was illegible. She had discovered this photo in amongst other family photos that her mother had passed on to her. She had thought that this was Bowdens Farm but oddly it didn't look like the image on Google.

Leaving the rolling Dorset countryside, they were soon down on the Somerset Levels. Either side of the road were hawthorn hedges and gnarled and coppiced willow trees which hid deep, narrow-sided ditches, or 'rhynes' as the locals called them. These rhynes enclosed rich green pastures where black-and-white, predominantly Friesian, cows were quietly grazing.

Occasionally Claire and Ross drove through prosperous-looking villages with grey, stone-walled farms and houses. Finally arriving at Curry Rivel, they took a left turn and arrived at the hamlet of Hambridge. Another left turn and they were there. Yes, it was the large square-shaped house that Claire had seen on Google. It was clearly occupied but it did not look like the photo in her pocket.

"This can't be the Bowdens Farm that we are looking for," she said disappointedly.

"Well there are Bowdens Farms all over the place," said Ross. "Never mind, let's go into the restaurant and have some smoked eel for lunch!"

Lunch was accompanied by a very good bottle of French wine. After an excellent meal and in high spirits, they visited the antique shop next door to the restaurant. Claire was smitten by a beautiful, circular, walnut, eighteenth-century table and just had to have it. She was normally quite thrifty, but there was something about the whole day and the ambience of the place that made her act in this uncharacteristic manner!

This was just the first of their jaunts down onto the Levels in search of the Uttermares. A few weeks after the tipsy lunch at Bowdens Farm, the graveyard at Drayton was visited. The very first tombstone on the right, after going through the gate, proved to be that of Claire's Great, Great Grandparents, Richard and Honour Uttermare. Later there were visits to the graveyards at Curry Rivel and Curry Mallet, where they found lots of Uttermares all resting in peace!

Another time they met up with Claire's second cousin, Clive, a newly discovered member of her family. The purpose of the meeting was to visit the church at Langport and to photograph those famous plaques that Sandy had talked about. Clive mentioned that his cousin, Liz, and her half-brother, David, now living in Canada, were also researching the Uttermare family tree and later Claire got in touch with both by email.

Liz and her husband came and had lunch with Claire and Ross later that summer. Claire felt an immediate bond with Liz. It was a family thing she supposed. The men hit it off too, rambling round the garden, whilst the girls chatted 'Uttermares'.

Claire, inspired by Liz's enthusiasm, spent quite a few of the next year's winter evenings, researching the Uttermares with the help of the internet. Coming across the name of a hamlet called Middleney on a census record, she had a 'lightbulb moment' and realised that that was what her

Grannie had written on the back of the old sepia photo. So, off she and Ross went to look for the house in the photo. On the map, Middleney was just a bit further on than Drayton. They arrived in torrential, driving rain and found what almost certainly was the house straight away. They sat in the car waiting for the rain to stop.

A villager walked by with her dog and looked curiously at them. "Can I help you?" she enquired.

They explained their mission and she surprisingly replied, "Well, I do know that a family by the name of Mead used to live in that house many years ago but talk to the chap who lives there now. I will introduce you to him. Come with me."

So, they met a rather eccentric, middle-aged man who was only too happy to show them around the old house. He was not at all fazed that they had turned up on his doorstep out of the blue, and he was pretty sure that the Meads, who had been prosperous farmers, had lived there in the past. From her research Claire knew that the Meads had continually married into the Uttermare family and vice versa.

The Meads had been prosperous yeoman farmers, as had the Uttermares. They lived on adjacent farms, and Claire understood that, through their marriages to one another over many centuries, their tenure of the land increased and became more secure.

Claire now knew where the Meads had lived, but what of Bowdens Farm that she had glimpsed in a bit of a tipsy haze following a boozy lunch last spring?

Once home again, and taking a deep breath, she phoned the number for Bowdens Farm that she had found on the internet.

A teenage girl answered. Claire explained the reason for her call, briefly outlining the fact that she was tracing her family history and that her family had once lived at Bowdens Farm.

"Best to talk to my uncle Henry Lang. He'll know all about that. He lives at Home Farm next door to us. Do you want his number?"

"Yes please, thanks very much," replied Claire.

"Nothing ventured, nothing gained." thought Claire, and she phoned him that instant.

Henry Lang turned out to be charming. He was really interested in what Claire had to say about the Uttermares.

"I have an old wheat sack in my barn with W. Uttermare printed on it, and the initials W.U. are carved into the beam above our kitchen fireplace and they are also on the lintel over the barn door. What's more, I've got lots of old Uttermare wills in my loft!" Almost as an afterthought he added, "Why don't you come over one evening? We are not too busy now the harvest is in."

Claire could feel her heart thudding with excitement as they fixed a date for the visit there and then.

Two weeks later, Claire and Ross turned into the drive of Home Farm just as the sun was setting over the surrounding Levels. The farm was immaculate. All the gates and fences were pristine and the large lawn surrounding the house had the appearance of a bowling green. The paintwork of the house and barns was freshly painted in the grey/green colour which was currently so fashionable. The house itself was old - very old. Claire guessed probably mid-seventeenth or maybe even sixteenth century. It was square and pretty, and built of the local grey stone - not the yellow, honey-coloured stone from the ham stone quarry near Yeovil that Claire was used to seeing in many of the Somerset villages.

Henry Lang was already at the back door and greeted them warmly. "Come in, come in," he said leading them into a beautiful, modern kitchen. The old inglenook fireplace was still there with a huge, blackened beam over it, but it now housed a gleaming red cooking range.

A pretty woman, who introduced herself as Annabelle came towards them. Like Henry, she was really interested in the story Claire had to tell them about the Uttermares who, it would seem, had lived in this old house almost two hundred years earlier.

"Well," said Henry, "from your research and with the evidence that I have, it would certainly seem that William Uttermare lived here all those years ago, but before we all get too involved with family history, what would you like to drink? Would you like to try our cider? The Langs have been brewers here in Hambridge forever."

So, Claire, Ross, Henry and Amanda tippled cider and talked Uttermares and Langs. Claire felt that she had always known the couple but, feeling rather merry, forgot to ask half the questions regarding the Uttermares that she had rehearsed in her head.

Henry showed them the clearly etched initials of W.U. on the oak lintel above the open inglenook fireplace and then led them outside to the barns. Henry was obviously a collector of old agricultural machinery and anything appertaining to the history of farming. There were old tractors, threshing machines, grinding stones, cider vats, brewing equipment and, of course, William Uttermare's 'wheat sack'. It was all worthy of a museum, but Henry shrugged and said it was just his hobby!

Leading them back into the kitchen, he indicated a pile of old documents on the counter which Claire, in a quietly inebriated state, had not noticed before. With a swift action Henry divided the documents into two piles. “These are Lang wills and these,” he said, pushing the second pile towards Claire, “are Uttermare wills. They are of no use to me, and you can have them with pleasure.”

Claire was thrilled and delighted.

Then, just as they were leaving, almost as an afterthought, Henry said, “Did you know that Home Farm was ‘gifted’ to the Langs - my family - by the Morrishes, who in turn were bequeathed it by the Uttermares?”

Well, this was indeed news to Claire. “Who on earth just gives very valuable property and lands to folk who are not related to them?” she asked herself. Her next thought was, “There must be a story there!”

Claire spent many of the following evenings reading through the wills - which were indeed old, dating back to the early eighteenth century. They were a dirty yellowy-brown colour, crumbling at the edges, and they had an unpleasant, musty smell. As she fearfully opened them with a wrinkled nose, she knew she was the first person to look at them in over three hundred years. Sometimes bits of old flies, wasps and spiders fell out of them and a fainter heart might not have pursued the project. She opened each in turn and, in her notebook, wrote down the names of the family members and to whom, and from whom, money, land and objects were bequeathed.

Gradually, she came to see how all these people were related - who was a father to whom, who was his brother, who was his wife, etc. Then she compared the Uttermares from the wills, to the Uttermares she had found on the plaques on the walls of the churches at Langport and Hatch Beauchamp. To her delight she found the names matched. The people on the plaques were the same people as those in the wills! It was like the pieces of a jigsaw puzzle all falling into place.

These people had been wealthy and notable. In 1722 John Uttermare had purchased the Lordship of the Manor of Hatch Beauchamp. His son, and subsequently his grandson, inherited the title and described themselves as yeoman farmers. They had married into the Michell and Bampfield families who had been lawyers and surgeons. Another Uttermare had been a Deputy Lord Lieutenant of Somerset, an appointment and honour bestowed by the reigning monarch.

The last William Uttermare, who had given Home Farm to Edward Morrish, had obviously lived there, but census records of the time referred to it as Wiltown Farm. Claire knew from her internet research, and from what her Grannie had written on the scrap of paper inside the lid of the brass milk jug, that members of her own branch of the family had lived at next-door Bowdens Farm.

The more Claire researched her family history the more questions she found. She was determined to answer them. In a large, hard-backed notebook which she had last used for revision of her physio finals in 1970, she wrote down her questions and answers regarding the Uttermares.

Part 2

Chapter 3 – Questions from Claire's Notebook

"When and why did the Uttermares come to live on the Somerset Levels and what were their origins?"

The Uttermares were an old Somerset family living on the Somerset Levels. The surname is now extinct globally but it is still to be found used as a middle name.

The name is thought to have two meanings:

The first originates from the Dutch heraldic name Uttermarsch meaning, 'one who dwells by the marshy ground' - as indeed they did.

The second originates from the French, 'd'outre mer,' meaning 'from beyond the sea' - possibly referring to a foreigner from France or Belgium, from where the name seems to have been imported.

"When did the Uttermares arrive on the Somerset Levels?"

There is no evidence found of them being here in Saxon times - more research needed on that.

The first record found is of Lieven Uttermeere born 1447, from Brussels in Belgium. The name Uttermeere seems to have changed to Uttermare by 1650.

Lieven may have settled at North Curry. He may have been associated with Flemish weaving, glass making or tiling. This was the end of the medieval era, Henry VI was on the throne, and the monasteries were at the height of their power. They were responsible for the drainage of the

Levels at this time. Lieven was possibly fleeing persecution from his homeland as a Jew or even as a Huguenot.

Received family wisdom suggests that the Uttermeeres came to Britain in or around 1688/89. They were said to be Dutch folk, accompanying William of Orange who had been invited to take over the throne of England. They were thought to have come here to teach the locals how to drain the Levels. At this time, the Revocation of the Edict of Nantes (1685) had been signed by Louis XIV, expelling thousands of Huguenots from France. They went to Holland, USA and five hundred thousand came to Britain. Many came here because Britain would have provided them with refuge under William of Orange, the new Protestant King. However, records show that the Uttermeeres, or Uttermares as they became known, had been living on the Levels long before this and were already well established as yeoman farmers by the late seventeenth century.

The drainage of the Somerset Levels started in Roman times and was continued in medieval times and mentioned in the Domesday Book. It was mainly carried out under the direction of the monasteries of Athelney, Muchelney and Glastonbury. Then, in the early seventeenth century during the reign of James I, there were abortive plans to drain Sedgemoor on the Levels. James's successor, Charles I, sold the Crown Interests, and the whole plan was taken over by Sir Cornelius Vermuyden, a Dutch drainage engineer. However, the Civil War and 'local opposition' had interrupted the project by 1638. Therefore, there were only six years of direct Dutch influence on the Levels and, as has been pointed out before, there are many records of Uttermeeres or Uttermares living in North Curry, Curry Mallet and Isle Abbotts long before this date. It is possible, of course, that members of the same family did come across with the Dutch at this time but, so far, there is no evidence for this.

The 'local opposition' to draining the Levels was from the local people, who had common grazing rights on the low-lying lush pastures of the Levels during the summer months. Traditionally, when these pastures became flooded in the winter, they and their animals would retreat to the drier slopes of the Polden hills, or even to the higher ground of Athelney and Muchelney which became islands in an inland sea.

Once drained and enclosed, this land would inevitably be taken over by richer farmers, so drainage was always opposed by the 'Commoners'.

- *The name Uttermeere had changed to Uttermare by 1650.*
- *By 1673 many of the Uttermares were calling themselves 'yeoman' farmers.*
- *John Uttermare purchased the Lordship of the Manor of Hatch Beauchamp in 1722.*
- *The Uttermares became landowners of their own land and leaseholders of lands belonging to the Duchy of Cornwall.*
- *The wills of these later Uttermares, donated by Henry Lang, were found in the loft of Home Farm, Curry Rivel.*

"Why did the Uttermare name die out?"

The Galton-Watson process states, 'If the average number of a man's sons is one or less, then their surname will almost certainly die out. If it is more than one, then there is more than zero probability that it will survive for any given number of generations.'

The military deaths on the tree are not Uttermares but come from the Pyne family (aristocracy) and the Banfields (legal family), in other words the upper classes. The Uttermare family tree showed that, indeed, the male survival rate was very low and did bear out the Galton-Watson process!!

"How were Richard Uttermare (born 1827, died 1913) and his wife Honour Uttermare née Mead, (my great, great grandparents) related?"

My mother told me that they were cousins but at what level of the family tree were they related?

Looking at the family tree it appears that the common ancestors were John Uttermare (born 12 March 1723) married to Honour Lovibond (born 23 October 1727). They were Richard and Honour's great grandparents, therefore Richard and Honour were second cousins. However, a birth record for Richard Uttermare (born about 1754, died 1840) has yet to be found. It would be the missing link.

"Who was the last Uttermare?"

The last Uttermare was Thomas Mead Uttermare born 1869 died 1949. He was the only son of Richard and Honour Uttermare, my great, great grandparents. He was a bachelor and had no children. When his father gave up farming, he took over Bowdens Farm and farmed it for a while. By 1919 he was found to be living and farming at Churley Farm, Stoke St Gregory. He is buried in the church yard there in the same grave as his niece Eunice Maud Louise Mead born 1900 died 1993. She was therefore 31 years his junior. She was the daughter of Fred and Lilia Mead who are buried in the same family plot. Thomas left five thousand pounds and seventeen shillings to Fred and James Uttermare Mead. There are still Meads living at Churley Farm to this day.

All Claire's research into the Uttermares was carried out during the winters. It had started in 2018 with the 'Beast from the East'. Now, in the winter of 2020 with the silent arrival to the world of Covid 19, Claire felt her research coming to an end. She had answered many of the questions that she had asked herself. She feared that there that there would now be a void in her life.

She and Ross had spent the first lockdown, from March 2020 to the end of June 2020, at home. The weather had been glorious - the spring bringing bright, sparkling days. Nature seemed to mock the secret deaths of so many human beings. The countryside had never looked better, and wildlife thrived. Claire spent that spring and the summer gardening and riding Mon Amie in the company of a new sixteen-year-old friend, Charlotte, and her horse Jimmy. There was little traffic, and they roamed far and wide.

Lockdown ended and so Claire and Ross decided to 'make a break for it' and headed to their house in France, visiting their children and grandchildren in Lyon on the way. Claire took all her family history notes with her, to tidy up loose ends. She decided to frame the finished Family Tree and bought a secondhand frame from a market stall in the nearby seaside town. It did look super when it was finished.

"Well done!" said Ross, as he looked over her shoulder at it.

"Thanks," replied Claire. "But wouldn't you love to know more about the lives of some of those Uttermares? I really would!"

Gazing at the Family Tree, now proudly hanging on the wall, her imagination took flight. She would give herself a bit of poetic license. Wasn't that what all historians did?

Sitting down at the round, cork-oak table, with her physio finals notebook, now transformed into her family research notebook, open at a blank, clean page, she looked up and out of the huge, shuttered French doors to the balcony beyond. Dreamily, she regarded snow-capped Mount Canigou in the far distance, gleaming like icing on a cake, in the sun.

Then her gaze shifted downward. Her pen took off, carrying her far, far back, into the mists of time.

Part 3

Chapter 4 – Leiven Uttermeere

Born 1447 in Brussels

A weak, wintery sun rose over the River Senne on a March morning in 1467. Its rays squeezed through the window slats of the old, shuttered house, revealing the outline of the young man sleeping curled up on his wooden bed. He stirred in his sleep, waking briefly, remembering that today was going to be different from any day that had gone before in his young life. Then he drifted back to sleep.

His name was Leiven Uttermeere and he was twenty years old. His 'given' name Leiven, meant 'dear, beloved friend' and Uttermeere, his family name, probably meant, 'he who dwelt by the marshy ground' - as, indeed, he did.

His parents had fled to Brussels from Spain some years before his birth. They were Sephardic Jews who had been persecuted for their faith by the Catholic Church. Many Jews had been forced to convert to Catholicism, but others, not wanting to do this, had continued to practice their faith in secret, whilst outwardly professing Christianity. They were known as Marrano Jews, a somewhat pejorative label. The Uttermeeres were the latter. Leiven's father was a master tiler, leaving a prosperous business behind in Spain to begin again in Brussels.

Brussels was ideal for the needs of a tiler looking to expand. The city was built on an island in the middle of the River Senne, with swampy ground on either side. The river was navigable from this point, and thence to the coast beyond Antwerp. The clay of the riverbank was perfect for tile-making and the river provided a means of transport for goods to foreign parts. Over the years a busy port had developed, the quaysides lined with both stone-built and wooden houses - some thatched, some tiled. Here merchants and tradesmen set up shop. This area comprised the lower town and was the working-class quarter. It was here that Leiven's father settled. Here he built his kilns for firing the tiles that would be bought by the rising merchant classes.

The town on the higher ground of the island was where the wealthy lived. It was surrounded by defensive ramparts, towers and fortified gateways. They enclosed a massive central square with a grand town hall on one side and a magnificent cathedral on the other.

Brussels became a rich centre of art and culture. Its diverse craftsmen produced wonderful sculptures in wood, huge tapestries depicting historical and religious scenes, ornate jewelry, and various plate and metal goods.

It was here that Leiven was born in 1447 in the already old timber-structure house that his parents now owned. The tile production had done well, as many of the growing towns and cities throughout Europe needed craftsmen of all kinds following the ravages of the bubonic plague of the previous century which had decimated the workforce.

From an early age Lieven had helped his father and his few labourers with the preparing and shaping of the clay. Tile making was seasonal. The clay was dug out from the riverbank in the winter and allowed to 'weather' until spring and summer, when the tiles were made, glazed and then fired in the kilns.

By the time he was sixteen, Lieven knew exactly how to cut and mould the clay. He learnt the new technique of making floor and wall tiles which were so much in demand for the great monasteries, cathedrals, palaces and grand houses of the time. The latest innovation was the production of 'two-colour' tiles. These were produced by inserting white coloured slip clay into the red clay of the tile body. After firing, the white clay became yellow, and the red clay turned a deep reddish-brown.

Leiven proved to have a good eye. He would choose to decorate the tiles with simplified floral patterns or, at times, to depict mythical creatures such as gryphons. Yet again he might portray fish such as pike that he had seen caught in the river. At other times he used the white slip clay to draw a figure or a scene from the old scriptures of the Torah that his mother had taught him. He found it comforting to think that they would be recognised by Christians as they knelt in their cathedrals or churches to pray. They would know them of course from the Old Testament of the Bible. Occasionally too, he had the conflicting thought that these same Christians were the same folk who persecuted his own people.

Waking from sleep, Leiven leapt out of bed and, in two bounds, was across the room knocking at the door of the adjoining bedroom.

"Time to get up Brother Philip," he called softly through the door. Hearing only muffled protests he pushed the door open, crossed the room, and shook the sleeping figure in the bed. A large, naked man pushed back the rough covering and swung his stout legs over the edge of the bed. He would have had a good head of red hair, but his head was the tonsured one of a Benedictine monk.

"Very well, very well, my boy. I know you are eager to be off. I will be down directly. I am sure your 'Maman' will have a good breakfast ready for us."

Brother Philip had only come into the lives of the Uttermeere family two evenings before. Leiven and his parents had been sitting having their evening meal when there was a controlled knock at the door. Leiven's father cautiously got up and opened it. They couldn't be too careful these days, especially as they lived along the Brussels quayside and all types from all over the world were to be found there. The middle-aged man standing outside was very obviously a monk. He wore a dark wool habit with a leather belt around his waist and leather sandals on his feet. Over his habit was a garment called a scapula, which was like a tabard with a hood or cowl attached.

"Monsieur Paul Uttermeere?" he asked in very correct French but with a pronounced English accent. "I have been told that you are a master tiler, and I would like to order some tiles for my Abbey at Muchelney in the West of England - well, Somersetshire to be precise."

Leiven's family spoke the local, historically Dutch language, which was something like Flemish. However, they understood and spoke French, as they had daily contact with French people who passed along the river and the roads of Brussels.

"Come in, come in," said Leiven's father reverentially ushering the big man in. "Do join us, there is plenty for all," and he indicated the huge oak table littered with cheese, hunks of cured ham and round homemade loaves. Leiven's mother, Mary, a kindly woman, looked rather surprised, but just thought to herself, "Well that's men for you! They think food can be magically conjured up from nowhere!"

The monk introduced himself as Brother Philip. He explained that the reason he spoke French was because he came from a noble Norman family called the Pynes. They had arrived in Somersetshire soon after the Norman conquest of England. The present King was Henry VI and French was the language of the court. Philip had been raised to speak French as well as the local English. However, he explained that he had rebelled against his family's expectations that he would become a courtier and man of influence. He had had a revelation from God, that he should renounce the privilege and wealth of his family's class and live a simple life, serving God and the peasants.

Leiven and his parents felt their hearts warming to him as he spoke.

"But" he added. "The reason I am here is business."

He explained that he was from Muchelney Abbey situated on the Somersetshire marshes. It had been founded by a Saxon King in the year 800 but had fallen into disuse over the next two or three centuries. However, Benedictine monks arriving in 1200 had started to rebuild. Now the present Abbot was in the process of expanding and renovating the Abbey. The Benedictines had become very powerful and wealthy in England and had money enabling them to carry out works like this.

The Abbot had seen tiles in nearby Glastonbury Abbey and wanted the same for Muchelney. He wanted floor and wall decorative tiles, and he would need roof tiles too. However, there was still a shortage of tilers in England as the Plague, or Black Death as it was known, had decimated the English workforce a hundred years before.

"So," he continued, "having made enquiries, the Abbot found out that the tiles he liked and had seen at Glastonbury Abbey had come from here. I will need to take back a good many tiles as an example of your work, and I need also a good tiler to come back to Muchelney with me to make tiles on site, and to teach the local people how to do it."

Leiven could feel his heart beating wildly. He wanted to be that 'good tiler'. He was ready for adventure!

"Let me go with Philip, Papa," he cried. His mother looked sad, but his father just nodded slowly saying, "Yes lad, it's time for you to spread your wings."

And so, that early spring morning saw Leiven and Brother Philip supervising the loading of the chosen crated tiles into one of the small craft tied up at the quayside. Once done, they climbed aboard and stowed their belongings and a small amount of food, under leather hides in the prow of the boat. This is where they would seek refuge from the elements for the next seven days. It would take them that long to sail down the River Senne, past Antwerp and thence to the North Sea via the River

Scheldt. They would be taking advantage of the spring tides which would help them on their journey down the rivers to the open sea.

The owner of the small sailing craft, Piet, was its sole helmsman and sailor but he expected Leiven and Philip to help with mooring, loading and unloading. Paul and Mary Uttermeere had come to the quayside to wave them farewell. Mary choked back her tears, not knowing if she would ever see her dark curly-haired and olive-eyed 'boy' again.

"Au revoir!" shouted Leiven to his parents as the small craft rounded a bend and they were lost to view. The journey to the sea passed quickly with a steady wind behind them. Along the riverbanks, they passed many windmills which were needed to produce energy for the newly thriving workshops of the region. They could also see large fishponds cut out in adjacent meadows, irrigated by the river, producing carp and trout for the local markets.

At night they would anchor and tie up at popular moorings. Here were to be found small hamlets where they could reprovision. Also here, were local inns or auberges, where they could spend the night if they wished - which they sometimes did, as the little craft had no cabin or wheelhouse in which to shelter.

Finally, they arrived at the heaving and very busy port of Antwerp. Ships, boats and craft of all kinds jostled for position, and the shouted orders of sailors and merchants filled the air.

"Be ready to moor up here, alongside this herring buss," shouted Piet to Leiven and Philip.

"D'accord!" Leiven yelled back, as he expertly slung the mooring ropes out over the side of their small sailing craft whilst Piet skillfully brought it alongside the much larger vessel.

Herring Buss circa 1480

The herring buss was made of wood and was about twenty metres in length. It was known to be a nimble ship, and very seaworthy. It had two masts with a square rig on the main mast.

"Do you know," said Philip to Leiven, "this boat looks a lot like pictures of Viking long ships that I have seen in books in the library of Muchelney Abbey back home."

Piet, overhearing them, agreed and added, "But this has a very different use! Nowadays, it leaves here at the end of May, with a fleet of four hundred others of the same, and heads north to the Hebrides to follow the herring shoals. The boat is used during the winter and early spring months to export all sorts of goods to foreign parts including Britain. It's a profitable little ship. But - enough of the geography lesson, let's get this lot on board before it gets dark!"

That night Leiven and Philip slept underneath the gallery of the herring buss. Early next morning they were awakened by the noise of the moorings being untied. Soon the boat was sailing in the middle of the River Scheldt and, quickly, they were out in the open sea.

The herring buss made good progress running before the wind, heading south, in the English Channel. After four days it sailed closer to the coast and then suddenly, changing tack, it headed westwards and rounded Land's End. Then, changing tack again, it headed North, battling the ferocious Atlantic gales on its port side. It was a relief to all aboard when the boat tacked once again and entered the quieter waters of the Bristol Channel.

The captain of the herring buss was a skilled navigator and was now looking for the entrance to the River Parrett which lay in the Bridgwater Bay halfway up the coast on the starboard side. It was spied by a young sailor who had climbed up into the ship's rigging. The herring buss altered course again and made for the mouth of the river.

Either side of the muddy, brown river were mud flats. Rounding a corner, the town and port of Bridgwater came into view. The herring buss moored along the quayside. Now all the cargo had to be unloaded and, if it was to be taken further up the river, it had to be loaded into flat-bottom barges moored at the town bridge. From here to Langport, the river was only navigable using these types of boats.

Philip was glad to have his feet back on home soil. "Not far now," he reassured Leiven, as they watched the precious tiles being lowered down over the side of the ship into the bottom of a barge. Waving and thanking the captain of the herring buss, they too clambered aboard. By midday they had reached the quayside at Langport.

Brother Philip was delighted to see his old friend, Brother Francis, waiting patiently beside a couple of stout Shire horses harnessed to a large wooden wagon.

"Hey up Philip! It's so good to see you again," Brother Francis called, as Philip leapt out of the barge and gave his friend a warm hug. Brother Francis continued, "I'd heard tell a ship was making its way up the estuary and did wonder if you might be aboard. You're safely back - 'tis an answer to all our prayers."

The precious cargo of crated tiles was hauled up onto the wagon along with bottles of French wine, copper pans, pewter plates and spices for the Abbey kitchens. Brother Philip had purchased all these en route for transportation by the herring buss - which would, in turn, pick up wool and cloth from Bridgwater to take back to Antwerp. English wool was of very high quality and much in demand by the rapidly expanding merchant and monied classes in Belgium for making their fine clothes and weaving the most beautiful of tapestries.

They were soon bumping along a very muddy, pitted trackway which was bordered on both sides by a deep ditch, or rhyne as it was known. The far side of each rhyne was lined by the gnarled trunks of pollarded willows and, through their green lacy branches waving in the afternoon breeze, Leiven could see flat, marshy ground extending to the horizon.

After two or three miles the land gave way to a slight rise and, between the trees, Leiven saw smoke rising from thatched, timber-framed houses. A little beyond them was a large, stone-built parish church. Rising behind the church he could make out the taller, more imposing outline of an altogether grander building.

"Welcome to Muchelney Abbey," cried Brother Philip. He was so glad to be back to what he considered to be his home. The Abbey was now being restored by the present Abbot, his monks, and a team of local labourers.

Climbing wearily down from the wagon, Leiven supervised the unloading of his tiles. Philip gave instructions that they be stored in a nearby barn.

The Abbot, a kindly man, was delighted to have Philip back and welcomed Leiven warmly.

"I'll have a look at these tiles that you have brought me tomorrow, but you both look tired and, may I say, somewhat bedraggled, so go and see what they can find you to eat in the kitchens. Leiven you are welcome to use the spare room upstairs as your sleeping quarters." Then he added a cautionary note. "I see from your name and by your looks that you are of Jewish heritage. You will need to be careful here as the King, Henry VI, is not kindly disposed towards your people, although we have no trouble with any of that in these parts."

"I quite understand Sir, but it's no problem, I come from a tradition of Marrano Jews, and we are used to keeping our heads down. I know the Christian ways and can recite the Latin Creed with the best of them!" he chuckled.

Brother Philip had acted as interpreter for this exchange between the Abbot and Leiven but, being young and bright, it would not take Leiven long to become fluent in the local Somersetshire dialect.

Next morning the Abbot, William Crokethorne, looked at Leiven's tiles and declared them to be perfect for the job of tiling the floors and ceilings of the Monastery.

"But we will need many more than that," he explained.

"Well Sir, that's why I have come here. Brother Philip says that you are short of master tilers due to the Plague and my father has taught me everything concerning this trade. I would like to start as soon as possible, and, with your permission, I would like to build a kiln next to the river but away from the thatched cottages where a spark could set fire to them. The lias clay of the banks of the River Parrett looks highly suitable for tile-making and I can find plenty of brushwood hereabouts for fires for my kiln."

"Go ahead my son, and may God prosper your work!" replied the Abbot.

Two weeks later, Leiven had built his kiln. Two-thirds of it was below ground and one-third above. It was too late in the year to cut out clay, but Leiven had plenty of work to do laying the tiles that he had brought with him. He needed help with his work to carry tiles and to mix mortar and, if he was going to expand his business, he would need to teach others his craft. He would need an apprentice.

The latter appeared in the form of Peter Mead, a fair-haired, blue-eyed young man of Leiven's age.

"Been sent to help you by Abbot William," he called out using a Saxon form of old English that was not unlike the German that Leiven understood and had often heard spoken back home in Brussels.

"I live over there," he continued, indicating the outline of a very large farmstead beyond the Abbey and parish church. This was the demesne farm. It had over one hundred acres of land, and its outbuildings and barns were owned by the Abbey. The present tenant was Thomas Mead, who had a large, rumbustious family who happily filled the thatched, timber-framed house.

Peter added amiably, "I've got two brothers, and me sisters help on the farm too, so me fether can spare me. Anyway, I don't much like all that cow muck and me fether do think I be a bit of a girl as I do prefer to draw."

"You sound just what I am looking for," chuckled Leiven. "We'll get straight to work and move all these tiles from that barn over there and stack them in the nave of the Abbey where we will be laying them."

Leiven and Peter got on famously together, and by Whitsun had almost completed tiling the floor of the nave.

Whitsun being something of a holiday, the village was buzzing with activity. The fair had arrived. There would be much carousing and merry making. There was always maypole dancing on the village green, and the girls and lads had been taught from an early age the intricacies of weaving the ribbons as they danced in and around each other. It was a holiday from work for all, and Leiven was invited by Peter to the midday meal at the demesne farm to meet his large family. Later in the day, all the villagers would come together on the green.

The family sat around the enormous oak table, dressed in holiday attire and in festive mood. Leiven had, of course, come across some of the Mead family before, such as when 'the girls' had been delivering milk to the Abbey kitchens, or when he had seen 'the boys' driving the cows out to the meadows. They were an extraordinary family in that 'the girls' were twins as were 'the boys. However, neither pair were identical twins and, in fact, Hester and Rachel were in all ways very different from one another - as were James and Paul.

Muchelney Abbey, English Heritage

Two medieval English floor tiles - Mid 13th to early 15th Century

Hester had long, red-gold hair braided in a plait around her head, and hazel-green eyes and fair skin, whereas Rachel had a mane of lustrous dark hair, dark skin and olive-brown eyes. They were both seventeen years old and stunningly beautiful but completely different from each other, physically as well as in character. Hester was lively and full of fun and quite talkative, whilst Rachel was more reflective and loved to read.

Unusually for the time, all the Mead children could read and write, having been taught by the monks at the Abbey. Many other people in the village were not literate, so the family were fortunate that they were Abbey tenants. The Benedictine community and the folk living in the villages for miles around were of mutual benefit one to the other. The Abbey became prosperous, receiving rents and tithes from the locals, who were cared for in turn, and ministered to, by the monks. The Abbey kept everyone in employment and enjoyed widespread local support. The Abbott was heard to say, "We live off our own you know."

The 'boys' were two years older than their sisters. Even though they were not identical, you could tell that they were brothers. James, the eldest by fifteen minutes, was tall, broad-shouldered and dark, whereas Paul, the younger twin, was inches shorter but also dark and swarthy. Both had olive-green eyes. The two of them were intensely practical and good with their hands.

They worked on the farm helping their father and today, which was May Day, was significant for them. It was officially the end of winter, and they had driven the cattle out of the barns in the early morning and down onto the summer pastures below the higher ground of Muchelney.

This was an age-old tradition for herdsmen on the Levels. Every winter the low-lying fields either side of the River Parrett would flood and so the cattle had to be driven up onto higher ground. This 'higher ground' included the islands of Muchelney, Athelney, Middleney, and Thorney. The 'ney' ending meant 'island' in old English.

Leiven was not the only guest at the meal. Brother Philip had also been invited, as he, Peter and Leiven had all become good friends over the last months. It was a noisy meal with everyone looking forward to the afternoon and evening revels.

By mid-afternoon when Leiven, Brother Philip and the Mead family arrived at the village green the festival was in full swing. There were stalls around the edge of the green selling wares and goods - local cheeses, vegetables and cider. The vendors were shouting out raucously to the crowded throng. Two pigs, or hogs as they were known, were already being turned on a huge spit by a couple of swarthy, young farm hands, their naked torsos glistening with sweat in the very hot afternoon sun. There would be quite a feast later that evening with free food for all.

Two huge bonfires had been built on the green, but care had been taken to site them safely away from the thatched roofs of the village houses.

“What are they for?” Leiven asked Brother Philip. He had asked the right person, because Philip had read and heard much about the old Pagan ways of the folk in these parts.

“Well, you know, Leiven, the old Britons - the Celts - they named today ‘Beltane’. We Benedictines and other Christians call it May Day or Whitsun. They would light the fires to please their gods and spirits. They would drive their cattle between the two huge bonfires and run between and around the fires themselves. Sometimes they would throw off their clothes and do this - their naked bodies illuminated orange in the firelight. It’s also said that once the fires had died down, they would run and dance barefoot through the glowing embers and ashes.”

“People here are not going to do that today are they?” Leiven asked worriedly. He didn’t relish the idea of going nude and dancing over hot wood ash, although, with enough cider inside him, he thought he might be able to perform well enough!

"No, no, have no fear. You know those old Celts had quite a different attitude to life and to love than some people today."

"What do you mean?" asked a wide-eyed Leiven.

Phillip replied, "There are new ideas circulating in Europe now, and they are receiving support and attention here. They are the ideas of a man called Martin Luther. He and his followers are against the excesses of the Catholic Church and its 'loose morality'. Whereas, the Celts or Britons had a very lax, or some might say healthy, attitude to life and sex. At Beltane they would send their young pubescent folk out into the countryside with the explicit purpose of exploring each other's bodies and of practising lovemaking. Sounds like fun eh!" added Philip, with a knowing wink to Leiven who had reddened slightly.

The focus of attention that afternoon was the maypole dancing. Leiven and Philip sat on bales of straw and armed with huge flagons of cider, watched the Mead 'twins' perform the intricate dance moves with the other village lasses and lads. They were very impressed, their eyes firmly on the graceful girls. Leiven was already smitten with golden-haired Hester, and Philip was completely entranced by dark-limbed Rachel.

As the evening shadows crept over the village green, the maypole dancing gave way to country dancing, with a fiddler and piper providing the music. The girls must have been aware of the intense interest they had provoked in Leiven and Philip because, whispering together, they approached, and pulling them up by their hands cried, "Come on! Your turn now! It's easy, anybody can do this!"

Leiven proved to be stiff, and not a natural dancer, often getting in a terrible muddle with the dance moves. When this happened, no one minded. He just received good-natured slaps on the back from the other young men. "Ye'll get the hang of it one day!" they joked. However,

Philip, despite his black habit, was incredibly light on his feet and Rachel was delighted to have him as her partner.

There were quite a few of the other Brothers from the Abbey present and even the Abbot appeared in time for the feast of hog roast, pies and sweetmeats all washed down with local mead and cider.

Some couples slipped away into the orchards next to the Green with just a nod and a wink from the older villagers. The spirit of their ancestors was alive and well tonight! By now the bonfires had been lit and the young children had been roaring round them - screaming and yelling with delight. Incredibly, some of the young boys had torn off their clothes, obeying some primeval urge. Their parents laughed and clapped at their children's antics, no one minded. This is what always happens on May Day night they mused.

It was nearly midnight when Leiven and Hester too slipped off together towards the beckoning orchards. Philip and Rachel stayed talking long into the warm night. Rachel, who was a good listener, found him fascinating. He knew so much about so many things but showed a humility as he expressed himself. The difference in their ages did not seem to matter, she just seventeen and he a mature man of thirty-seven. As well as being intellectually in tune, there was a huge physical attraction between them. Feeling and becoming increasingly aware of this, but being torn by his calling, Brother Philip said, "I think it's time we both went home, don't you"?

"Oh! My parents won't mind!" she protested. "They know, and can remember, what happens on May Day night!"

"That's as maybe, but my Abbot will only turn a blind eye so far, and it's early morning vespers for me in a few hours." Reluctantly they went their separate ways.

Much later, Leiven and Hester too parted reluctantly. Leiven just knew that this was the girl for him and for always.

As they recrossed the now almost deserted village green, their arms entwined around one another, Leiven said "So we'll be married then, shall we?"

"Yes," she giggled. "But you must ask me fether first."

To the delight of everyone, Leiven and Hester were married in the Parish church of St Peter and St Paul one month later. It was arranged that they should live in a cottage at North Curry, belonging to the Abbey, which was just a few miles by footpath across the water meadows from Muchelney.

Meanwhile, Philip and Rachel continued to see and talk to each other. The Abbot and all the other Brothers knew what was going on but chose to ignore it.

Although the Abbey prospered, things were somewhat lax. The restoration of the Abbey went on apace - the gardens, fisheries and beehives were all well-maintained and cared for by the monks; vespers and prayers were all observed and said at the correct time - but there was a very relaxed air to the place and a non-judgmental attitude prevailed.

Philip and Rachel fell deeply in love and, not long after Leiven and Hester's son Jan was born, Rachel gave birth to a boy that she and Philip named Benedict.

Rachel's parents were very accommodating, and she and Benedict, lived in the demesne farmhouse alongside all the Mead family. Philip was a regular visitor. Benedict grew up helping on the farm with the cattle, learning from his uncles. He also learnt the scriptures from his father and was observed to be a very spiritual child.

Chapter 5 - Jan Uttermeere

Born around 1468

So it was that Jan Uttermeere, son of Leiven, and Benedict Pyne, son of Brother Philip Pyne, were born in the same year of 1468. They were cousins and grew up together in the village of Muchelney but their lives were affected by the course that history was about to take, and this led to widely divergent paths.

Jan Uttermeere worked alongside his father, Leiven, learning the tile trade. Over the years most of the tiles laid in Muchelney Abbey were the work of Leiven, Jan and Peter - who was now also an accomplished tiler. However, very sadly, Jan's first wife, Mary died in childbirth and their little son with her. Jan was distraught and didn't marry again until much later. He was sixty-two when he married Maud in 1529 and in 1530, she gave birth to William.

Benedict Pyne, although happy enough working on his grandfather's farm, felt God's call. He was still a young man when, one day, he felt compelled to go and seek out the Abbot. He opened his heart to the old man, saying that he felt very conflicted, not knowing what he should do. Taking him into the Abbey garden in the spring sunshine, the Abbot outlined the Bible to him, explaining things from the Fall of Adam through to the Resurrection of Jesus Christ.

As the Abbot spoke, Benedict felt an amazing warmth wash over his body, and he perceived an intensely bright silver-white light all around him. The Abbot finished speaking and led Benedict back inside the Abbey. Nothing more was said, and Benedict made his way back to the farm. He hardly uttered a word for the next few days. He felt he could not speak.

Two days later Benedict knocked on the door of the Abbot's quarters. "Come in my son," called out the Abbot. "You've come to join us haven't you. I felt it here," he said indicating his heart.

Benedict was accepted into the order, taking vows of 'Stability', 'Fidelity' and 'Obedience' with only 'Poverty' and 'Chastity' being implied. It meant giving a lifelong commitment to the Benedictine community at Muchelney to ensure that the Brotherhood would endure.

For the next thirty-five years Benedict lived the life of the Benedictine Order. Everything was to be done in moderation, be that eating, sleeping, reading, working or praying. It meant, in reality, that the Brothers lived a very normal life, taking part in the day-to-day activities of the Abbey and village community, whilst still attending to their spiritual lives as well.

Over the years the Abbey remained extremely prosperous. This was due to the support and the good husbandry of its tenants and, under the good guidance of the present Abbot, William Wyke, the Abbey was now almost complete.

However, all this changed dramatically when, in 1538 the King, Henry VIII, was excommunicated by the Pope. Henry pronounced himself head of his newly formed 'Church of England'. He thought that the monasteries had become too rich and powerful, and he set out to destroy them. He put Thomas Cromwell in charge. Cromwell sent out Royal Commissioners to carry out Henry's wishes.

One day, a team of these men arrived unannounced at the doors of Muchelney Abbey. Brushing aside the objections of the Abbot and the Brothers, they proceeded to make meticulous notes of all the Abbey's possessions, which included all its gold, silver and fine vestments. They demanded to know what rents were paid to the Abbey and what property and land was owned by the Order.

Then they issued their ultimatum to the Abbot and the Brothers.

"You will all leave the Abbey and renounce this way of life. If you do not obey this order from King Henry, you will be known as heretics and will suffer the consequences," adding the warning, "We will be back."

A time of confusion, weak leadership, and downright skullduggery now prevailed within Muchelney Abbey. Bribes were paid to the Commissioners and thence to Thomas Cromwell to ensure that one young and able monk named Dan Ynde should be ordained Abbot. In return he and other like-minded monks would leave when the Commissioners next returned, but with certain guarantees for their future.

All this horrified and saddened Benedict. He was determined that he would not comply with the Commissioners, whatever the punishment. His opinions and feelings were well known within the Abbey, and he would probably have to pay for them with his life.

A few weeks later, Jan Uttermeere and his men were putting the finishing touches to the cloister walls when a loud knocking was heard at the massive oak front doors. The Commissioners were back.

The Abbot, the Prior and eight monks all assembled in the Chancel, some, including Benedict, kneeling and praying on the tiled floor.

"We have come to demand that you surrender in the King's name!" the Commissioners bellowed to the rather cowed group.

The Abbot, Dan Ynde, stepped forward. "We will comply with your demand as long as we have your assurance that we will be found new positions in the New Church or given pensions if we are deemed too old to work." He knew full well that this had been the deal when he had bribed them earlier.

"I don't surrender to you or the King," shouted Benedict, getting to his feet. "My loyalty is to this monastery, to the vows I have taken, and to God".

That did it. He was grabbed, punched, sworn at and knocked to the ground. His wrists were tied behind his back, and he was pushed roughly into one of the nearby cells, normally used by the monks for prayer and contemplation.

"We will deal with you later, and you know what to expect!" the Commissioners bawled at him. He most certainly did know. There had been graphic stories reaching the Abbey of abbots and monks up and down the land who had held out against their torture. They had had no proper trial, and many had been executed. They had either been burnt at the stake, as was the case with the devout Abbot of Glastonbury, or hung drawn and quartered.

The Commissioners started their work that very day, collecting up all the gold and silver plate, fine tapestries and vestments, and cash from the safe. All this was to fund King Henry's potential wars against France, for which he needed to build a huge navy.

They loaded all their 'loot' into wagons and, leaving an armed guard, went off to the local ale house to drink and whore the night away. They would be back the next morning, to harness their heavy horses and transport the stolen goods to London, taking Benedict with them. They would deliver him to be 'examined' - a quaint name, for the rack or whatever other wicked instrument of torture they could think of.

However, they had not counted on Jan Uttermeere and his men who had witnessed what had happened to Benedict.

"Come on lads!" Jan urged them. "We have to get him out of there."

The Abbot and the other monks were not about to help them, they had long gone!

Hauling up a stout tree trunk, recently felled, they used it as a battering ram to break down the oak cell door, and Benedict was quickly freed.

"You must get away from here quickly," Jan told him. Benedict protested but finally they persuaded him that he was of more use to the world spreading God's word elsewhere, rather than staying here, and ending up as a bloody corpse, with his head on a spike and his body parts decorating the entrances and exits of nearby villages.

As the afternoon light faded, they smuggled him over to the demesne farm where he changed into peasant garb. The plan was, that he would seek refuge at Pitney Manor, ten leagues away - the home of the Pynes, his Grandparents. He had never met them, but he would throw himself on their mercy.

Jan's son William, now aged eight, had been helping with the evening milking and it was agreed that he would lead Benedict across the marshes between the tall reeds, following ancient tracks.

Meanwhile, the guards that the Commissioners had left to guard the richly laden wagon, had found some of the local mead in the now deserted kitchens. They got very drunk, sitting propped up against the side of the wagon in the warm evening sun. They had heard the splintering of wood nearby but had chosen to ignore it for a while.

Finally, reluctantly, one of them staggered to his feet, hazily thinking that maybe he should investigate the noise. He swore loudly when he discovered the beaten down door. He also noticed that there was no sign of the tiler and his men who had been there earlier. He reckoned rightly that they had been responsible for liberating the prisoner.

"Come on!" he yelled to his mate. "We can catch them if we hurry, or there will be hell to pay!"

In an inebriated state and leaving the wagon unguarded, they set off into the village. Grabbing an old, stooped man who was quietly collecting wood for an evening fire, they demanded of him, "Have you seen the tiler who works in the Abbey?" The old chap pointed vaguely in the direction of the demesne farm.

Attempting to run on what felt like leaden legs, they could see, beyond the farm, one large and one small figure, at the far end of a very large meadow. These figures disappeared into the lower moorland.

The moor was made up of tall reeds, known as withies. The locals used them for weaving baskets and caskets and other useful things that were needed for rural life. There were tracks through the withies that had been used since the Stone Age. They were constructed on raised causeways and had treacherous boggy marshes on either side. It was through this that William, who knew the marshes intimately, was leading Benedict.

The guards started to gain ground, and Benedict and William could hear the footsteps and heavy breathing of the inebriated men not far behind them.

Coming to a place where the withies were less dense, William whispered to Benedict, "Go straight on. The road to Pitney lies one league ahead," and he watched as the large-framed man plunged into the reeds on the opposite side of the clearing.

William hid himself on one side of the track, taking out his sling shot and deftly loading it with a surprisingly heavy, round, smooth, grey pebble that he had collected from the shallows of the River Parrett. He had a good aim and would often bring home pigeon, moorhen or wildfowl for the pot.

The first guard crashed clumsily into the clearing. He never knew what had hit him and he went down as if he had been shot. The second man stopped abruptly and, seeing his mate lying completely still, bent down to take a closer look.

"Well, he's not breathing and there's not a mark on him," he thought to himself in a befuddled way. He had heard about the ghosts and spirits that lived in these marshlands and, being a superstitious man, he was filled with terror. He turned tail and ran. Unfortunately, being blind with alcohol and fear, he crashed off the track and into the bog. Screaming, the poor man was sucked beneath its muddy surface.

William made his way back to the demesne farm, and recounted to his father, Jan, and to all the men, what had happened. Jan, like his father Leiven before him, was an intelligent fellow with a razor-like intellect. He could foresee problems ahead, and his brain quickly formulated a plan of action.

"Listen boys," he said. "The first thing we must do, is to get rid of thick ere body lying on the track. We'll just heft him into the bog with the other bugger. The mud will soon suck him under."

Detailing two of his men for the job, and looking directly at his son, he added, "And you mun go along wiv 'em an show 'em where it be to". His Old English, Somersetshire dialect became broader as he excitedly gave out instructions.

"The next problem we have," he said, "is that, when those Commissioners come back tomorrow morning, they are going to find the guards and their prisoner gone. If we go back to the Abbey now, and put on another cell door, those townies will never know the difference. We shall hide the wagon in the farm barns, and we can divide up the 'loot' between ourselves. Then we will all be there when the Commissioners arrive and we will tell them that, as we left the Abbey to come home this evening, we saw the guards helping themselves to gold and silver coins. We will say that we challenged them and told them that we would report them. At that the guards had fled, wagon, horses, loot an all!"

Next morning when the Commissioners returned, slightly hung over, they found a group of village men at the door of the Abbey. Jan told them the story. The Commissioners looked at the cell door and, finding it unlocked, pushed it open and found the room empty.

The oaths they uttered in that holy place were terrible. "How did this happen?" They looked accusingly at the now-grinning men, who were hardly able to contain themselves.

"Well," said Jan, "Have ye read yer Bible? Have ye read the story of how St Peter was led out of prison by an angel? Well, you know it was a very holy man that you imprisoned here. I wouldn't be surprised if," and his voice just trailed off.

The three Commissioners began to tremble and turn pale. Saying no more, they pushed their way past Jan and his men and were last seen walking dejectedly back to the village. Whether or not they got a sympathetic hearing from their royal masters on their return to London, the villagers never heard!

The two stories - the one of Brother Benedict, and his escape from the cell at Muchelney, and the biblical one of St Peter - got mixed up in the minds of the local people. The legend of St Benedict, who miraculously escaped from the clutches of King Henry Vlll and Thomas Cromwell, and who disappeared into the marshes on the Levels, is still talked about to this day.

Chapter 6 - William Uttermeere

Born around 1530 married Agnes Bridges born 1530 died 1562
William, as a child, spent much of his time on his great grandfather's farm, where he adored being with his two great uncles, James and Paul. When he grew up, he had two strings to his bow. He had become an apprentice to his father, Jan, who was a master tiler, and he was also to be found working with the cattle in the lower pastures of the demesne farm at Muchelney. The latter occupation was his first love.

As he grew up, he witnessed the destruction of Muchelney Abbey. Much of it was looted by the villagers and gentry alike, who took the stone from its walls and tiles from the roof, for their own use. Jan and William were commanded to take up tiles they had previously laid in the Abbey, and to re-lay them in the parish church.

The demand for tiles had diminished because most of the abbeys in England had been destroyed. However, Jan and William still had orders from the parish churches and from the great houses. For this work, they had to travel far and wide but they both preferred to stay in the local area around Muchelney.

Jan passed away one cold winter. He left his profitable tile business to William, who subsequently, now having the chance to indulge in his passion for farming, sold it, and acquired the leasehold of one hundred acres of prime pastureland at North Curry. This made him, by definition, a yeoman farmer. All the land at North Curry had long been owned by the Duchy of Cornwall.

He was a good dairyman and prospered. Like many of the Uttermeeres he had inherited his grandmother Hester's flaxen hair and hazel-green eyes, but he had the strong, square build of his grandfather, Leiven.

By the time he reached twenty-one, the age of consent, he was still living at Muchelney with his family, but farming his own land at North Curry as well. From time to time, he received some rather direct comments from his mother, such as, "Well 'tis about time that ye found a wife of yer own, to cook and clean for ye, t'wood give me a bit of peace fer a change."

William could take a hint. He used to go to Langport cattle market every Saturday morning, driving his old and surplus stock along the wide droves which were lined with lacy-leaved, graceful willows, but which were hiding deep, and often treacherous, rhynes. Butchers, farmers and traders from far and wide would bid for, and buy, his much-loved cows, calves and bullocks.

Market day was the highlight of everyone's week, and by the time William and his men had herded the cattle into their pens, the rest of the market was in full swing. The noise was terrific, as was the stench coming from the animals. There were fowl and duck cooped up in cages, and pigs, goats and sheep, in makeshift pens and stalls.

Once the auctioning and the bidding for the cattle was over, William was free to enjoy the day. He meandered amongst the stalls, and then lingered over a tankard of cider whilst sitting outside the ale house chatting to all the local lads.

Out of the corner of his eye he spied Agnes Bridges, a pretty girl of nineteen who was helping at her family's stall. He thought he would buy his mother one of the reed withy 'dollies' that Agnes had made, and which were meant to keep away evil spirits. Maybe it would stop his mother grumbling at him!

He chatted amiably to Agnes. Choosing his moment, he invited Agnes to tea the next day, not knowing if this would suit his mother or not.

Of course, Agnes accepted his invitation, and they often met after that.

Six months later it was agreed they should marry. They did not need the permission of her father, as they would have done in earlier, and even in later, generations and everyone said they were a good match.

Agnes's family, who came from Langport, had no qualms about her marriage taking place in North Curry church. It was known as 'The Cathedral of the Levels' and had a certain cachet. Agnes's mother, a loud woman and something of a snob, was only too happy that her daughter was to marry this well-off farmer, and that the wedding feast would be hosted by his family at his new farm at North Curry.

Agnes's father was not concerned either. He was always too tired after his day's work of manual labour to bother his head with his daughter's wedding plans! He was the overseer of a team of river labourers who manhandled barges around Langport Bridge. Although the bridge had nine arches, the river flowing under them was too shallow to allow boats to pass underneath unaided. His family had done this job for many generations, hence their name of Bridges.

His bossy wife took charge of their daughter, Agnes. "Have you decided what you are going to wear for your wedding?" she demanded.

"Don't worry Mother," her usually compliant daughter replied. "I've got it all worked out in my head. I'll wear my bluey-grey, woollen, 'Sunday Best' kirtle, with my best linen shift under it. I want my hair done in braids in a loop around my ears, and I'll wear a fillet net around the crown of my head with a white linen veil over that. And I want my bridesmaids to wear the same as me."

"Well, that all sounds good, but have you and William fixed a date yet?" asked her mother in a rather belligerent way.

"Yes, it's to be the twentieth of January next year, after the banns have been read three times out loud at the Church of St Peter and St Paul in

North Curry. I know you are going to ask, 'What's the hurry?' and 'Why have a wedding in the depths of winter?' but it's a simple answer - we just can't wait any longer!"

"And what will you use as flowers?" asked her mother huffily. "Not many around then you know."

Agnes again had her answer ready. "Thought of that! There will be plenty of snowdrops under the hedges. I may even find some Lenten roses blooming and we will find plenty of holly and ivy sprigs with which we can decorate my kirtle belt, and I'll put snowdrops and early primroses in my hair."

It snowed during the night of the nineteenth of January 1549, so when Agnes awoke next morning, the fields were glistening in the bright sunlight, and she knew the flooded Levels would be frozen solid. There would be skating and sliding on them later.

All the preparations had been done. The women had spent the previous day preparing sweetmeats, bread, pies and jellies. Duck, moorhen, and even swans, were now all cooked, and decorated with their feathers. The men would be responsible for making sure there was enough ale and cider to go round. There was to be a hog roast too. The trestles had been set up in one of the barns and anyone who could play an instrument would be welcome to turn up and play for the dancing. The same band would accompany the bridal procession from William's farmhouse to the church, being joined on the way by most of the villagers. Everyone would stand during the service, there being no seating in churches at that time.

All went according to plan and William wore his 'Sunday Best' too. Agnes had never seen him looking so grand, almost like one of the local lords, except his doublet, breeches and hose were made of wool and his box-pleated neck ruff was made of linen. He also sported a new pair of knee-length leather boots.

They made a fine couple standing before the alter taking their vows. It was a wonderful day and everyone wished them a long and happy life together.

They prospered and had children and grandchildren. Over the next three generations, the Uttermeeres continued living at North Curry, working as farmers and butchers.

During that time there were huge social and religious changes. The Crown passed to Henry VIII's young son Edward, who was happy to go along with the Protestant ideas of his father. Next in line was his sister Mary, or 'Bloody Mary' as she was called. She was a Catholic, who truly lived up to her name, burning innocent people for their faith. Then it was young Queen Elizabeth's turn. She reverted to, and upheld Protestantism, but she too, had no truck with anyone she considered a traitor. She had died by the time that William's great grandson, John Uttermeere, known as 'the Elder' was born in 1615.

Chapter 7 – John Uttermeere the Elder

Born 1615 died 1709
John Uttermeere the Elder was born in 1615. He married Ann, and together they farmed and brought up their family at North Curry. However, with the growing rift developing between King and parliament, their quiet existence on the Levels was about to change significantly.

Charles I was on the throne when John and Ann married. He was an ardent Catholic who believed in the Divine Right of Kings and was unsupportive of his parliament. The Crown and the Church were seen to be too wealthy and powerful by many, and Protestant ideas were gaining ground and circulating amongst the working and merchant classes. Oliver Cromwell, a staunch Protestant, organized troops and declared war on Charles, his army and his supporters. It was Civil War, pitting Englishmen against each other - even brother against brother and father against son.

So, on an early spring morning in 1644, a twenty-nine-year-old John Uttermeere was to be found moving around his cattle stalls, making sure his animals were all looking their best in readiness for market in Taunton later that day. These cattle were a mixture of young stock and old barren cows - all surplus to his requirements - that had been bred and raised on his farm.

He had inherited the right to farm much of the land that his forebears had farmed, and lived in the same house that his father, grandfather and great-grandfather had occupied. He was possibly the most affluent person in North Curry and had a standing amongst the locals. Although young, his knowledge of the Levels was second to none, and his advice on farming matters was often sought, even by his elders. He was a real giant of a man with muscular, tanned limbs and a shock of thick, flaxen hair inherited from his five times paternal grand-mother, Hester.

He stood, leaning over the wooden cattle stall, musing about events going on in the wider countryside. From time to time, a peddler selling his wares would pass through the village, and in the summer, groups of pilgrims on their way from Muchelney Abbey to Glastonbury, came that way. All had stories to tell of the conflict raging between Oliver 'Ironside' Cromwell and their glorious King Charles.

They told of how an opening battle at Edgehill, had taken place, up country in Warwickshire, two years earlier in 1642. It had been inconclusive. The two sides had unexpectedly found themselves very close to each other and so were forced to engage, although neither side really had the heart for a fight. The King's army turned up late in the day to face Cromwell's men. Both sides were ill-trained and ill-disciplined, and many ran away to loot each other's baggage trains. The King was allowed to escape back to London where he was denied entry by Parliamentary forces.

Since then, John had heard tales of outbreaks of violence and looting between opposing factions all over the land, including here in Somersetshire. Why, only last week his neighbour, Samuel Coat, had told him that some drunken Royalists, or 'Cavaliers' as they were known, had ridden into his flock of sheep and driven them into a nearby rhyne. They had killed a couple of them, dragging the carcasses behind their horses, no doubt for a feast of mutton that night. There was nothing poor Sam was able to do about it.

There were worse stories too, of the wives and daughters of village folk, being violated by both the Parliamentarians, the so-called 'Roundheads', and the Cavaliers. With this last thought in his head John went into the house.

"Have been thinking," said John addressing his wife Ann, and his three sisters. They were Agnes Webber and Marie Larcombe, both married to farmers, and twenty-one-year-old Jayne who was engaged to a local blacksmith, Johnnie Dyrham. They were all helping with the day's cooking, as their men would need feeding when they returned from Taunton market with John.

With a furrowed brow John continued, "When you go down to the fields to milk the cows, or when you are just out and about on the farm, I think you should arm yourselves, because these so called 'soldiers' that are roaming the countryside, are becoming bolder and more dangerous by the day. A knife tucked down the side of your boot would be a good idea."

"I've always found a knee in the groin works well," chuckled Ann. Jayne pretended to be shocked.

"Well, don't say I haven't warned you," grumbled John. "We'll be off now." And he ducked his huge frame under the low doorway leading into the yard.

He whistled up his dogs and mounted his horse, Meg. His men were already herding the cattle out from their stalls and into the lane leading towards Windmill Hill. The dogs worked well, keeping the cattle to the middle of the track and preventing them from straying too near the edges of the deep rhynes that were on either side. If a cow were to fall in, a huge amount of effort and time was needed to get them out again.

It was eight miles to Taunton, and it would take two or three hours to reach the marketplace. John rode in front on Meg, with his men and dogs to each side of the herd and to the rear. Periodically, they were joined by other herdsmen and their stock. The huge throng of men and animals wound its way onto higher ground after leaving the Levels. Plodding slowly up Windmill Hill, they then descended into Solomon's Hollow - a wooded glen.

About a mile away from Taunton, John felt Meg quiver beneath him. The horse snorted loudly and put her ears back flat against her thick poll.

“Something wrong old girl?” John whispered to her, patting her neck reassuringly. Then he heard it - musket fire and cannon too!

Holding up his arm, John twisted in his saddle and shouted to his men, “Trouble ahead, I think. Take it slowly now.”

Taunton Castle came into view, and then it became obvious what the ‘trouble’ was. Encamped below the castle walls was the Royalist Army, besieging the Parliamentary forces and the townsfolk inside the town. Woodsmoke drifted eerily from the encampment towards John and the herd, and the sound of gunfire and human voices was carried to them clearly on the wind.

“There be no market for us today I fear,” shouted John. “Those buggers won’t let us through I know!” Almost before he had finished giving his instructions to his men to turn the herd around, five Cavaliers came galloping across the open ground towards them.

They wore wide-brimmed hats, adorned with bright feathers, rich silk tunics, and long leather-spurred, riding boots. They were whooping and hollering and brandishing swords and pistols. They were most likely drunk, thought John. He himself only had his riding whip and his clasp knife on his belt for protection, and anyway he had no wish to get embroiled in a fight! He had no opinions as to the rights and wrongs of either side, but he did want to protect his family and his property from the loutish behavior and looting of both the King’s, and Cromwell’s supporters.

“What arrogant bastards they are,” he thought to himself as the five Cavaliers rode at full tilt, cutting out six of his best beasts from the herd.

Laughing in his face, and jeering at his men, they drove the animals back to their encampment.

Feeling humiliated and worried for their futures, the whole gathering of men and animals wound their way back to North Curry.

That night, John, his workers, and all the other farmers and men who had been with him that day, assembled at the local alehouse. John stood up and addressed them.

"We have to protect ourselves." he started. "We must form a local defense vigilante force, to stop our wives and daughters being raped, and our crops, livestock and property being damaged or seized. We must prevent our young men from being forcibly conscripted by one side or the other, and we must stop those who threaten our lives in this hideous Civil War!"

He stopped, breathless, and then, almost as an afterthought, added, "And, so that we are known to each other, we will wear a white ribbon in our lapels. We will arm ourselves with whatever we have to hand - be it cudgels, flails, scythes, sickles or clubs!"

A young wag, leaning on the doorpost, pint pot in hand, shouted out, "Yeh, we'll call ourselves 'the Clubmen' fer 'tis what we'll do - we'll club 'em!" At that, there was an uproarious cheer of agreement.

For the next year the villagers of North Curry lived in fear. They heard terrible tales of what was happening up and down the country. Close at hand the town and castle at Taunton continued to be besieged, first by one side, and then by the other. John and his neighbours could no longer go to market to sell and exchange their animals and produce. There was increasing poverty in the countryside.

By now, Oliver Cromwell had formed a crack regiment called The New Model Army. It was highly disciplined and effective and under the command of General Fairfax. His soldiers were sent to Taunton to relieve the Parliamentarians, who were trapped in the castle by the Royalists led by General Goring.

John and the men of North Curry had witnessed at first hand the drunken, hooligan behavior of the Royalists, and were not surprised to hear that, once the New Model Army arrived, Goring and his troops had fled in the direction of Bridgwater, a Royalist garrison. They were untrained and disorganized, and had become strung out along the river Yeo, pillaging from the local people as they went. Many of their commanders were lax, with little or no control over their men. There were retreating, ill-disciplined Royalists, over a large area, much of it down on the Levels surrounding the farms and homes of the Uttermeere family.

Early in the morning of 9th July 1645, Johnnie Dyrham, who was shortly to wed Jayne Uttermeere, was beginning his day in his smithy in the village of Isle Abbotts. During the night he had heard gunfire, and so was expecting trouble from one side or the other of the warring factions. Sure enough, within a few moments, he heard the clattering of a horse's hooves on the cobbled yard outside. He could hear from the sound that the horse had cast a shoe.

A bedraggled and blood-splattered Cavalier slid down the side of his horse to the ground, demanding that Johnnie should shoe his horse immediately. Johnnie was not going to argue, especially as the arrogant man had thrown down some gold coin at his feet.

As Johnnie worked, the man told him that he was possibly the only survivor of a skirmish that had occurred during the night. He said that he was part of Goring's Cavalry, and that they had been sent off in this direction to draw the fire away from all the other troops headed towards Bridgwater. However, a crack troop of Parliamentarian cavalry had come after them, and completely routed them. The Cavalier blamed their commander, George Porte, who he said was useless and hadn't posted sentries for the night.

Finishing the job, Johnnie muttered, “Well, I do believe ye had a lucky escape. You’d best be on yer way. ’Tis my belief yer chances be slim if they catch up with ye.”

The man wearily mounted his exhausted horse and cantered off.

Hearing that there were troops from both sides all over the countryside, Johnnie thought it best to close the smithy for the day so that he could go and check on Jayne and her family over at North Curry, a few miles away. He swiftly saddled up his own reliable young thoroughbred, a beautiful chestnut mare called Morgan.

They set off at a good trot along the narrow tracks, which were bordered by deep rhynes and willow trees. He knew the way over this part of the Levels like the back of his hand. They were dry and passable now, unlike in the winter months when they would be completely submerged by floods.

Soon, he passed the site of the previous night’s skirmish, and the bile rose in his throat at the sight of at least sixty corpses strewn around in the summer pasture. What sickened him more, was that here, he could see his neighbours - men, women, and even children - bending over the bodies. They were taking whatever they perceived to be of value. Pockets were being rifled, arms and weapons taken, and even clothes were being unceremoniously removed and secreted away.

One man, Tom Larcombe, a tenant farmer of just a few acres, and married to Marie Uttermeere, came up to Johnnie grinning from ear to ear.

“Have ye heard? Them Roundheads of Cromwell’s have captured Yeovil, and all the King’s men are running like hell towards Langport. ‘Tis reckoned their commander, Goring, ’e plans to make a bit of a stand there. What’s more, the lot that slaughtered these poor buggers,” and he indicated the bloody corpses with a flourish of a magnificent, looted

Royalist sword, "they took off directly they had finished 'ere, and are headed for Langport too."

Johnnie made no comment, just wanting to be away to see that Jayne and her family were safe.

Arriving at North Curry, he found them all at breakfast. Everyone had stories of rogue soldiers from each side, marauding through the farmland, taking whatever and whoever might be useful to them.

"This is all getting very close to us," observed John Uttermeere. "I want all the cattle, sheep, and pigs, brought up from the meadows and put in the barns for safety. Arm yourselves as you go, and don't hesitate to use force to defend yourselves and the animals if needs be."

Johnnie, the rest of the family, and the farm hands set to and spent all day carrying out John's orders. By nightfall all the animals and farm implements had been housed in the barns. John ordered Johnnie and two of his men to sleep near the barn doorways, keeping the dogs with them for the night. He himself would sleep in the main house with his wife Ann, and his sister Jayne.

Unbeknown to any of them, the most decisive battle of the Civil War, would take place the following day, 10th July 1645, only seven miles distant at Langport.

Early in the morning of that day, General Goring, the Royalist commander, and seven thousand of his troops, had managed to position themselves on top of Pics Hill, one mile east of Langport town. Below them was a valley bisected by a deep rhyne, the Wagg Rhyne. On the opposite side of the rhyne and facing them, was Fairfax with Cromwell's New Model Army of ten thousand men. The outcome was never really in doubt.

There was a narrow lane, lined with bushes, leading down from Pics Hill to the ford in the valley bottom. It was, normally used by townsfolk to cross the rhyne. Goring chose to secrete untried Welsh foot soldiers in the hedges to provide cover. He only had two light guns to fire down the lane at the enemy opposite. He ordered three regiments of cavalry to wait on the ridge of the hill overlooking the small valley.

None of this was any defense against Cromwell's men. The Royalist guns were soon silenced. One thousand five hundred musketeers 'cleared' the hedges of the poor Welshmen, and then Cromwell's 'Ironsides' galloped, four abreast, up the lane. On reaching the ridge, they broke Goring's Cavalry. The last remaining Royalist Cavalry counter-attacked, but they too were completely routed by a charge of horses from yet another Parliamentary regiment. Then more Parliamentary reinforcements streamed up the lane and Goring's men broke and fled the field.

Their intentions were to flee as best they could in the direction of Bridgwater. The Parliamentarians were hot on their heels and, in a cowardly attempt to deter them, Goring and some of his men set fire to Langport. The Royalists were fugitives now, and it was every man for himself. Many looted and torched the houses of Langport and did the same to small cottages and farms as they spread out over the Levels. They were pursued by Cromwell's men, and many were attacked by the local 'Clubmen' who had banded together to defend themselves and their property against the armies of both sides.

During that day, John Uttermeere and his family were hearing reports from their neighbours of the battle that was taking place six miles away in Langport. The wind was blowing hard in from the coast and, from time to time, they heard distant cannon fire. All the animals remained in their barns for their safety, but the cows had to be milked as always. They would become uncomfortable and restless if left. So, at three o'clock in the afternoon, Ann and Jayne, pails in one hand and milking stools in the other, made their way over from the house to the barns where the milking cows were being kept.

Moving quietly, they placed their pails under the cows' udders and settled themselves carefully onto their three-legged stools. They both loved this work, placing their heads against the warm bellies of the cows and listening to the steady hiss of the stream of milk as it hit, first the bottom, and then the sides of the buckets. The cows chomped away peacefully on the plentiful hay in the troughs in front of them. Usually, the women chatted and laughed together while they milked, but today they were quiet and apprehensive. Their tranquil, largely uneventful lives were no more, and they lived now with the ever-present fear of danger.

They were jolted out of their somber reveries, when the large oak door of the barn opened and two disheveled, drunken soldiers stumbled in. They could have been from either side, probably both foot soldiers, and of low breeding.

"Look 'e what we have 'ere," cackled one as he lunged towards Jayne, who was nearest to the door. He roughly pushed her off her stool and she sprawled in the straw, screaming as she went. The man was on her in an instant.

The other man, who was older, threw himself at Ann, and she too was knocked to the floor of the barn. But she was ready for him, having seen his approach. As he came falling full length over her, she bought up her knee and hit him hard in the groin. As the man reared back roaring in pain, she reached down to the inside of her black leather boot, from which she deftly retrieved a very sharp kitchen meat knife. The man came at her again, but she was quicker than him and, reaching up, she plunged the knife deep into the side of his neck. He instantly fell back, spouting blood from his carotid artery. Ann knew she had killed him. She had seen pigs slaughtered like that often enough!

Scrambling to her feet, she was horrified to see Jayne being pinned to the ground by the other brute. He was stifling her screams with his hand and attempting to throw her long skirts over her head. Ann, still with her bloodied knife in hand, was about to use it when the man, sensing her presence, whirled round and knocked her flying.

At that moment Johnnie, who had been in the adjacent barn and had been alerted by Jayne's cries, crashed through the barn door. He was carrying his pitchfork, and, when he saw what was happening, he threw the weapon through the air like a javelin towards the man. It embedded itself in the man's chest, and he fell back with a terrible scream. Johnnie stood over him, hearing the blood gurgling in the man's throat, and seeing his writhing body. "Die slowly, you dog, that'll teach ye to violate our womenfolk!" he yelled.

Johnnie helped the ashen-faced women back to the house. It had been a terrible experience for them, but Ann was philosophical, saying to the assembled family, "All's well that ends well eh!" - an expression she had recently heard used at the local market, but she had not a clue from whence it came!

The next day, they heard from farmers over at Middlezoy that the local 'Clubmen' had had a meeting with General Fairfax, who told them that he and his men would, from now on, pay for all supplies they took from their farms. He said he would leave their families and farms in peace and safety, provided that the Clubmen did not assist the Royalists.

The Battle of Langport, or 'The Battle', as the Uttermeeres called it, was a decisive one for Cromwell and his army. King Charles no longer had any support in the West Country. He had hoped, misguidedly, to be able to rely on the country manors to supply men, food and equipment for his army. He now had support from only the Midlands and the North of England, and even that was sparce.

Peace descended on the Levels once more, but only for a brief forty years.

Charles I lost his head in 1649 and, in the same year, four years after 'The Battle', Ann gave birth to a bouncing baby boy and, of course, they named him John! His father was delighted, and decided it was time to increase his acreage. He wanted to provide well for his new, young son.

The draining of the Levels began in Roman times and had been continued by the monasteries but, with their dissolution, all that work ceased. Consequently, the Levels flooded every winter, and the 'Commoners' who had access to the rich pastures in the summer were forced to retreat with their animals to higher ground due to the rising water levels. They made the slopes of the Polden and Blackdown Hills and the islands, such as Muchelney and Athelney, their winter homes.

During the reign of James I, when John the Elder was still a young man, the process of draining and enclosing the Somerset Levels began again. This continued under King Charles I, who invited a Dutch drainage engineer, Sir Cornelius Vermuyden, to come and provide his advice and expertise. The drainage process was stopped in 1658 by the Civil War, and by 'local opposition'. This 'opposition' came from the 'Commoners' who rightly felt that they were being deprived of their livelihoods and their land. It was only the richer farmers and landowners who could afford to buy this newly drained and now very workable pasture.

Having become aware that land three miles distant at Curry Mallet had been newly drained and enclosed, John put in a bid to buy it from The Crown Interests, who owned it. His bid was successful. He farmed the land from home at North Curry, planning that when his son, John the Younger came of age, he would be able to take it over.

It was in this way that the Uttermeeres spread out over the Levels - many to be found living within the Parish of St Peter and St Paul at North

Curry, and others living and worshipping within the Parish of All Saints at Curry Mallet. Later they would be found further afield in the villages of Curry Rivel, Isle Abbots, Hambridge, Fivehead, and Drayton - all of which were within three square miles of each other. During these often very troubled times down on the Levels, these yeoman farmers didn't go far!

Chapter 8 – John Uttermeere the Younger

Born 1649 died 1709
On a bitterly cold winter's morning, in the year 1658, John Uttermeere, aged nine, and his younger brother made their way down the muddy track from their farm, which led to the centre of the village of North Curry. They were on their way to school.

Not many villages had a school and not many children were fortunate enough to go to one. However, some years earlier, the Lord of Hatch Beauchamp Manor, had endowed North Curry with a fine, stone-built school building. It had two school rooms, one for the boys and one for the girls, and a pleasant courtyard for recreation time. Schooling was not compulsory and many children attended infrequently and remained illiterate. This was the case with the Uttermeere children who were often needed to help on the farm.

Neither boy relished the day ahead, as their master was an unkind man and used his cane unsparingly. They filed into the cold classroom with the other boys and sat down on one of the long wooden benches, which were in rows across the room.

The older pupils, like John, were issued with hornbooks, which were wooden boards with a handle. Fixed to the board was a sheet of paper with the letters of the alphabet and The Lord's Prayer written on it. This was overlaid and protected with a thin, translucent layer of animal horn. It was a teaching aid that had been in use over the previous one hundred years. Each boy had a slate and a slate pencil to write with. Both the hornbook and the slate with its pencil had to be stored in the classroom at the end of the school day, as they were too precious to be taken home.

Mr. Jones, their master, entered, swishing his cane as he swaggered in. He was a fat, arrogant Welshman, who had come from a background in law and not from the Church - which was the more usual way of entering the teaching profession. There was a rumour circulating in the village that he had been involved in a legal scandal and accused of taking bribes back in Wales. Consequently, it could be deduced that he had made a run for it to the quiet, sleepy hollow of North Curry where no-one knew him!

All the boys hated him. They immediately stood up, dreading what was coming next.

Pointing to the first boy standing in front of his frightening and domineering frame, he bellowed, "What's yer name boy?"

"Isaac Worthy, Sir."

"Write it down," roared the master. The poor boy took up his slate, balancing it on his knees, and he began to write with his slate pencil. This could be rubbed out with a bit of spit and the cuff of his sleeve if he made a mistake.

"And you boy?" hollered the master.

"John Podger Sir," replied this lad, more confidently, starting to write.

Then it was John Uttermeere's turn. "And your name too boy?" shouted the master, leaning threateningly towards him.

"'Tis John Uttermeere," he stammered with his strong Somersetshire accent.

"What did you say? Speak up, or I'll box yer yers boy!" replied the master with his equally strong Welsh accent.

"'Tis John Uttermeere, Sir."

"Well write it down boy, don't just stand there."

“I..I can’t,” stammered John again. He had hardly been to school in the last two years and he did not know how to write his name. His parents couldn’t teach him as neither of them was literate.

The master nearly exploded with wrath. “Well, I’m not surprised you can’t write it. What sort of a name do you call that anyway? Sounds like a ‘Frenchie’ sort of name to me. We don’t want any of that ’ere do we? This is how you write it.” With a flourish, he wrote on his own blackboard, ‘JOHN UTTERMARE’.

“Write that down!” he shouted, staring at John with his horrible, piercing black eyes.

John did as he was told.

“Make sure you always write it so,” threatened the Master, “or you will pay for it,” and he brandished his cane menacingly in the air.

At the end of the school day, a tired and woeful pair of now ‘Uttermare’ boys trudged home. Their mother, Anne, knew there was something wrong by their downcast faces.

“What’s the matter?” she asked, and they told her the sorry tale.

“Well, ‘tis not right,” she said, going to the oak dresser and pulling out from its shelf the Family Bible. On the inside cover was written in beautiful script, ‘Leiven Uttermeere in the year of our Lord January 1st 1530.’

“You see,” she told the boys, “thick Lieven there, ’e were one of yer long ago Granfers. I ’erd it tell that ’e could write because ’is wife Hester, who were a Mead, had been schooled by the monks at the Abbey, yonder at Muchelney. She taught ’im to write and their children could write their names too. But, after the Abbey was destroyed by the King, people couldn't write nor read no more."

"Well, I be afeared to write it like that," replied John. "If I do, I shall pay fer it with a birch switch across my arse!"

And so it was, that the family name changed from Uttermeere to Uttermare during John the Younger's lifetime.

John grew up in a Protestant home. The Uttermares who, during the Civil War had claimed allegiance to neither side, now felt obliged under Cromwell's rule to conform to the Puritan 'norm'. The women of the household, John's mother and sisters, wore white linen caps, or 'coifes' as they were known, and brown or grey long-sleeved woollen waistcoats over long, dark, woolen skirts. On their feet, they wore stout, sensible leather shoes, which were the order of the day. On Sundays they wore this same outfit, but in black, which was seen to be 'showier'.

John, his father, and his brothers had short, cropped hair and, when going to church or market, wore black 'stove pipe' hats with wide brims. Also, when not working on the farm they wore dark leather doublets with wide, square white, linen collars and white cuffs, britches with garters at the knee, wool stockings, and leather shoes. Clothes were not to be flamboyant as had been the way of the previous Royalist establishment.

The Uttermares now had to give up some of the more 'Catholic' aspects of the Church of England and lead a more sedate life. They were also compelled to send their children to school with more regularity!

John left the village school at the age of twelve and went to work alongside his father on the family farm at North Curry. The farm was well over one hundred acres and had mixed stock. They also held the leasehold of land belonging to the Duchy of Cornwall over at Curry Mallet and, when John married Anne Newman his childhood sweetheart in 1672, he moved into the farmhouse that he, his father and their workers had built there.

The following year Anne gave birth to a lusty, dark-haired boy who, of course, was named John. He was known in the family as 'Young John' to distinguish him from his father, John the Younger, and his grandfather, John the Elder. In 1676 a daughter, Joanne, was born followed by another son, Richard in 1680.

On Saturday 21st June 1685, John Uttermare the Elder, aged seventy, his son, John the Younger, aged thirty-six, and his grandson, Young John, aged twelve, were herding their cattle along the droves to Taunton Livestock Market. They had heard that James, Duke of Monmouth and his now considerable army of local volunteers from the West Country, had reached Taunton. The Duke was intending to make it his headquarters, before continuing on to take London.

The Uttermares were not unsympathetic to Monmouth. Like the majority of folk in the West Country they disliked the present King James II, a Catholic. They remembered the awful persecutions under Bloody Mary and they were beginning to see similar things happening under James II. They had begun to enjoy their peaceful Protestant lives, and now feared this new King and his heavy taxes.

Entering the large marketplace with the cattle via the narrow streets was not easy. The locals had turned out to meet Monmouth, and four hundred men from Taunton had joined him already. Some of his army had been encamped outside the town, but many of them were in and around the big market square, looking for food and women. It was a dirty, smelly and dangerous place, with one area being used for the slaughter of bulls. The tradition was that specially trained dogs were kept that would attack the bulls, biting at their flesh to 'let' their blood. This was thought to improve the flavour of the meat.

Johnnie Dyrham, the farrier from Isle Abbots, was also there that day. Knowing there was business to be had, he had set up his forge to one side of the marketplace.

All at once, there was a surge of people moving towards the market cross, as it was noticed that two of the town's magistrates had positioned themselves importantly on its plinth.

"What's going on?" Young John Uttermare asked his father and grandfather who were marshalling the cattle into their usual places in the roughly made stalls. Unable to resist the lure of the crowd, the three pushed their way forward.

Then, from a side street, emerged a beautiful white horse, and riding it, was a finely dressed army officer. He was wearing a long, bright red coat embroidered with fine gold thread and, across his chest 'en bandolier', a fabulous royal blue silk sash. His hat was wide-brimmed, Cavalier style, adorned with red and white ostrich feathers, and his legs were clad in long, thigh-length leather riding boots.

"So, this is the Duke of Monmouth we've all been hearing about!" thought young John. His father was no less impressed and was filled with a longing to be up and away from the farm and join with the rest of his fellow West Countrymen in fighting for freedom and justice. A hush fell on the expectant crowd.

"We proclaim James, Duke of Monmouth, King of this realm," shouted one of the magistrates, and all the crowd cheered. Then Monmouth doffed his hat with a flourish and held up his hand commandingly. The crowd fell silent.

"Join me, men!" he cajoled them. "I will be a good King to you and your families. I will uphold your right to worship as you wish, and I will treat you with all fairness."

With that he was gone, phantom-like, back into the side streets leading to the outskirts of town, and to his army, now numbering about six thousand men. They had come from all over the West Country - Cornwall, Devon, Wiltshire, Dorset, and now Somerset. They came of their own free will. It was probably the first time in the history of Britain that this had occurred. Before this time, ordinary men would have had no choice and would have been sent to fight by their manorial lords or, indeed, would have simply been 'kidnapped' or conscripted to fight by passing armies. But these West Country men believed James Monmouth and what he was promising them. He was truly a very attractive and charismatic, young fellow!

By early afternoon the Uttermares were ready to head home. They had a successful day, selling all the cattle they had brought to market for a fair price and buying some good young bulls to improve the bloodline of their fine dairy herd.

Passing out of the market square they called out their 'goodbyes' to Johnnie Dyrham who was still busy at his makeshift forge. Johnnie called out to John the Younger. "Hey! A word if ye will," and John left the herd and went over to Johnnie, his brother-in-law.

"When ye get home, would ye go over to Isle Abbots and tell Jayne I be not coming home fer a while. I've been asked by one of Monmouth's men to go along with them as their farrier. They will pay me well and I don't have to fight neither!"

Johnnie knew what he was talking about. He was a member of the Royal Guild of Farriers. The profession was as old as Christendom. The Romans had employed farriers to travel with their armies. Not only did they shoe the cavalries' horses, but they were also equine vets. They were known as 'Immunes' and exempt from fighting.

Jan van Wyck (1652-1700) - James Scott, Duke of Monmouth and Buccleuch
Oil on Canvas, National Portrait Gallery, London

Simon Johannes van Douw (1630-1677) 'At the Farrier's'
Oil on Panel Private Ownership

Maybe not too surprised at this request, John replied, “Well, I can certainly do that fer ye. I really envy ye and would like to come with ye me’self, but I know me fether would not be best pleased if I up and left ’em all. It’ll be harvest soon enough, and it’s a busy time right now with all the young stock this time of year. Anyways, I wish ye well and Monmouth too. I really believe in what ’e is fighting for! May God bless ye and keep ye all safe.” And, with a rueful backward glance, he hurried away to catch up with the retreating cattle.

Next day, Monmouth, his huge army, and Johnnie Dyrham headed towards Bridgwater which had been a Protestant town since the Civil War. However, King James was now aware that his nephew, James, Duke of Monmouth, was gaining widespread support. To counter this, he sent his generals, Faversham and Churchill, with their well-disciplined armies, to harry and prevent any further progress of this rebellion.

Monmouth’s army didn’t stay long in and around Bridgwater, travelling first northward towards Bristol, where they were thwarted on the outskirts of the city by the Royalists. Then, turning east, they skirted south of Bath trying to reach the road to London. However, they were continually engaged in skirmishes with the King’s troops. The rebels began to feel discouraged; morale and discipline flagged, and many drifted back to their homes.

Monmouth thought it best to regroup and headed back towards Bridgwater. Johnnie, who had been kept busy shoeing horses and tending to their injuries and wounds, also judged it time to quit the scene. Anyway, he was missing Jayne and home comforts! Arriving back in Isle Abbots he found his cottage and forge deserted.

“You looking fer yer missus?” shouted his neighbour to him across the village street. “She be with ‘er family over at Curry Mallet.

Leaping back into the saddle, he galloped over the moor at a reckless speed. It was supper time when he arrived at the Uttermare's farm. All the family were gathered in the kitchen, sitting around the oak table, heartily eating cold ham after a hot day outside working in the sun. All were pleased to see Johnnie, although they noted how thin and bedraggled, he looked.

"Come and eat and tell us what ye 'ave been up to," encouraged John the Younger. Through mouthfuls of boiled potatoes, cold ham and beef, Johnnie told them of Monmouth's limited success and how he and his army had been held up and harried by the King's forces at every turn.

"Now," he said, "they be back in Bridgwater, I reckon."

There followed a long discussion around the table of the rights and wrongs of the campaign. They all supported Monmouth and his cause.

"Well," said John the Younger, "I suppose you, Johnnie, will be going back to join them soon to do more farriering, and this time I be coming with ye!" The women were aghast, but there was nothing they could do or say to prevent their men from taking off.

On the morning of 5th July 1685, John the Younger, and Johnnie Dyrham arrived in Bridgwater. That evening, a scout sent out by Monmouth, reported back that a large Royalist army had encamped at Westonzoyland behind the Bussex Rhyne on the moor. Monmouth decided a surprise, night attack would be the best tactic.

Johnnie Dyrham made his base on the higher ground outside the church of Westonzoyland. He knew he would be in for a lot of work during the night. He relished this, as it would mean that he would be well-paid and that he wouldn't have to fight!

John the Younger was mounted on his warm-blood, everyday farm horse, Jack, and was armed with a rather old-fashioned musket. He rode with a bunch of militarily, ill-trained horsemen who, rather like himself, were more used to walking behind a plough horse, than charging into battle atop of one.

"They don't stand a chance," mused Johnnie to himself. "There may be more of them, but they are no match for the well-disciplined King's men. But I guess a nighttime attack using surprise. whilst the enemy are either asleep in their tents or drunk on cider, might just work."

But it didn't. Someone from Monmouth's side fired a shot by mistake, and the King's men were instantly roused. It was a rout.

Being met by a battalion of well-trained Cavaliers, John and his fellow horsemen were in disarray. Poor Jack, frightened out of his wits, reared, threw John to the ground and took off southwards in the direction of the farm and 'home'. John crawled for cover but was soon rounded up with four hundred other men and marched, with hands tied, over the moor, up a narrow lane and into the church at Westonzoyland.

Conditions in the church were terrible. The prisoners, some with mortal wounds, were crammed into the small space. Nine of them died and nothing was done to help the wounded. John was not hurt, but he was bruised from his fall from Jack and had received a black eye from one of the Royalist men sent to guard them. He was horrified to find himself in this situation and was very afraid.

Johnnie had seen the bedraggled and bloodied men being marched into the church and had recognized John.

"I'd better get out of here," thought Johnnie to himself, "It's obvious our side is beaten, and it won't be long before they take me prisoner too. My being a farrier with 'immunity', will most likely mean nothing to them.

Mounting his horse, he headed north, making a wide detour of the whole area before returning home.

Next day, John and the surviving prisoners were marched, shackled, to Bridgwater, and thence to Taunton, where they were kept in squalor in the castle dungeons. How he survived that terrible march and subsequent imprisonment, could only be put down to his fitness from working on the farm, and his strong faith in God's protection.

Of course, it was Johnnie Dyrham who broke the news of John's capture to the Uttermare family. They had feared the worst when Jack had clattered into the cobbled stable yard with his stirrups flapping, reins broken, brambles in his matted mane, and horrible deep scratches down his flanks. He must have jumped many rhynes and hedges on the ten-mile journey back to the farm at Curry Mallet.

The family received more news of John's fate when John the Elder and his grandson, Young John, were next at the Saturday livestock market. They were given news that he was being held in the dungeons of Taunton Castle in filthy, murky conditions. On subsequent visits to the town, John the Elder took food and warm clothes to the gates of the prison and was able to bribe the guards into giving these to their prisoner.

Meanwhile, James II was determined that the 'good folk' of the West Country should be taught that the 'Crown' was never again to be challenged as it had been at the Battle of Sedgemoor. He appointed Judge Jeffreys, his Lord Chancellor, to go to the West Country to conduct the trials of the captured rebels. The trials were mainly held in Taunton although they also took place in other West Country towns such as Dorchester. It was widely known that these rebels would be accused of treason and condemned to death. However, it was also known that the only person who could commute the sentences was the King, using 'the prerogative of mercy'.

John the Elder was well-informed and knew all these facts. He knew also that sometimes, a big, fat bribe paid to a judge could sway the verdict. However, being a good Puritan, he believed that was not the way to do things. He felt he might be able to appeal to the King because he did know a few influential people, one of whom was Lady Elizabeth Bruce, née Seymour.

Lady Elizabeth had inherited Hatch Beauchamp Manor near Taunton and its lands in 1671 at the age of sixteen on the death of both of her parents. John had rented land on this estate for many years, and it was his son, John the Younger, who was responsible for the care of the dairy cows that grazed there. He and Elizabeth had become good friends as young adults, but it never went further than friendship - she, respecting his knowledge of the land and its animals and he, showing due deference to her station as Lady of the Manor. Now, aged thirty-six, John the Younger was languishing in Taunton Castle goal, and his father wondered if maybe Elizabeth could help.

It was well known that Elizabeth, as a young heiress, had spent a lot of time at the court of the King at St James Palace, Westminster. The Seymour family had a long history of being in and around the royal court. It was also well known that before, and even after, his marriage to the Queen, King James II had the reputation of being something of a libertine, and that Elizabeth had been one of his many mistresses!

Donning his Sunday best and making sure his horse was well-groomed, he sedately rode the three miles from his farm at North Curry to the Manor House, now rather derelict, at Hatch Beauchamp.

Elizabeth, now aged thirty, had married Thomas Bruce, the Earl of Elgin, at the age of twenty-one. She was a kind woman who had become matronly over the years, and she beamed a warm smile at John as he was shown into her drawing room. He bowed deeply to her as she asked him, "What can I do for you? It's been quite some time since last we met."

"It is Madam, and it's been bad times, I fear. I have come to beg a favour from you, as I know you have some influence with our King," and John explained the dire situation that his family found themselves to be in.

"Of course I will do what I can, but I am afraid I cannot promise anything," purred Elizabeth. "Now, tell me all about the family, and I'll order some tea, or maybe something a little stronger - you could probably do with it!" she laughed as she rang a little bell on an ornate side table.

Later, as John rode thoughtfully home, Elizabeth composed a letter to her former lover, King James. She begged him to have compassion for one John Uttermare, now being held prisoner in Taunton Castle goal, and due to come to trial very soon. She extolled John's virtues, saying he was a wonderful custodian of the land and a true Englishman, and she begged the King for mercy. She sealed the letter with the Seymour seal and called for her groom.

"Take the best horse and deliver this letter with all speed to King James's Palace, Westminster. You must personally place it into the King's hand. Let no other take it from you."

On 19th September 1685, Judge Jeffries arrived in Taunton from Exeter to continue with his bloody assises. Starting in Winchester, he had proceeded with his murderous, butchering ways, via such places as Frome, Salisbury, Dorchester, Lyme Regis and Exeter. All those found guilty, which were the majority, were hung, drawn and quartered - their limbs and torsos tarred and then placed all around the countryside on buildings, railings and gateposts to act as a deterrent to the locals.
Now he presided over the Great Hall of Taunton Castle. On 21st September the first four prisoners were brought before him. Instead of keeping their heads bowed they looked up, and when asked, "How do you plead?" they answered boldly, "Not Guilty!"

“In that case,” replied Jeffries, “you will hang!” and they were summarily executed.

Up to three hundred prisoners who had been kept in the dungeons, appeared before ‘The Hanging Judge’ over the next few days. All now pleaded guilty, and all would be executed in due course. Some would be hanged in Taunton and others from village hanging posts and trees. John Uttermare the Younger was among this number. By now he had lost a huge amount of weight, was filthy, and resigned to his fate.

However, what was not generally known, was that King James had demanded a list of names of all the captured rebels. It was he alone who decided the outcome of the guilty verdict that Jeffreys, who, as the King’s lackey, was bound to pronounce. At the King’s command eight hundred men were transported to Bermuda in the West Indies. They were sold into slavery to his ‘friends’ at between ten and twelve pounds per head.

At Taunton, three hundred men were executed by hanging, however twenty-four were pardoned. John Uttermare the Younger was amongst these fortunate few, thanks, one can only surmise, to the letter written by Lady Elizabeth Bruce, née Seymour to the King.

John had been waiting his turn to be taken outside and executed. Then a guard called out his name from a list of others.

“You men come with me,” he commanded, and they fearfully followed him up the dank, foul-smelling passageway to the dungeon’s outer door. “Right, you lot can go,” shouted the man as he released them from their shackles. “You lucky blighters have been pardoned by the King!” and with that he pushed open the door and they stumbled through it into the sunlight.

John and the others were taken care of by the townsfolk, given food and shelter, and treated like heroes. The news that he was free soon reached his family who quickly harnessed the wagon to Jack, by now fully recovered from his exploits on the battlefield at Sedgemoor, to fetch him back home.

John made a surprisingly good recovery following his ordeal. He gained weight, thanks to Ann's wonderful cooking. The fact that there had been an abundant harvest that year meant that they all ate well.

Now he was feeling so much better he took his two sons, Young John and Richard, aside and told them, "I had a lot of time to think while I was in prison. I want the best for you, so I want you to go to a good school. There is no such school in Taunton, so I have arranged for you to go to the King's School in Sherborne. You John, now that you are thirteen, can start next week as t'is the beginning of the Autumn term." Then, turning to little Richard, he said, "You will stay at the village school until you are eleven and then you can join your brother if all continues well here."

And so, Young John was sent to The King's School in Sherborne as a boarder. This ancient school, under the direction of Sherborne Abbey, was attended mainly by boys who were destined to go into the church. There was an emphasis on the learning of Latin and choral works. So, it was a strange choice, maybe, for the sons of a farmer.

As it turned out, by the time Richard reached the age of eleven, in 1691, his father had had a couple of bad harvests on the farm. Funds were low and Richard was sent to Foster's Grammar School, also in Sherborne, instead.

Foster's was a charity school which had been endowed, or founded, by a farmer from Boys Hill called Richard Foster and had opened only four years earlier in 1687. The school was known as the Blue School because the boys wore blue coats. They were also issued each year with a bonnet or cap, like a large floppy beret, two shirts, two cravats and two pairs of shoes.

The school had been founded only for boys from Sherborne and its villages but, because John Uttermare the Younger knew Richard Foster from market days in Taunton, strings had been pulled!

The completely different types of education that the two boys received led to differences in the direction of their lives, and to the lives of subsequent generations. Although both remained as yeoman farmers, it appears that Young John and his offspring associated with, and married into, the families of lawyers, surgeons and Justices of the Peace. Indeed, one became Deputy Lord Lieutenant of Somerset! Whereas Richard's descendants remained very closely rooted to the land, some as humble farm labourers and some as more prosperous yeomen farmers.

Chapter 9 – Young John Uttermare and Richard Uttermare

Young John Uttermare, born 1673 died 1766 (aged 93); Richard Uttermare born 1680 died 1726 (aged 46).

1691 had been a poor harvest year because, for much of the spring and early summer, a prevailing westerly wind had driven in 'mizzle' rain from the sea across the Levels. Neither the crops nor the Uttermare sheep - who provided a major source of revenue from their wool and their skins - had done well in the damp conditions.

Young John Uttermare, now aged seventeen and home for the summer holidays, had, as expected, put in a full day's work on the farm of his father, John the Younger, at Curry Mallet. His young brother Richard, now aged eleven, also worked as hard as any of the hired labourers that his father employed.

Now, with the harvest gathered in, it was time to return for the September term at Sherborne King's School, and Young John was looking forward to being back with his friends. He had missed the stimulation of classes. He loved Latin and French and was fascinated by the New Sciences. He also loved singing in the Abbey Choir, for he had a fine tenor voice.

However, he was not looking forward to having his young brother Richard, who was starting at the Blue School as a new boy, in the same vicinity. Having mixed with a higher social class - the sons of clergy, lawyers, aristocracy, and even the newly emerging 'nouveau riche' - he found his brother's Somerset accent and, what he deemed to be loutish behavior, tiresome and embarrassing. Richard, who was just a normal country boy, thought his brother something of a snob!

Early one September morning, they left the farm with their father, using the farm wagon pulled by a couple of the farm horses. It was already blustery, with sudden gusts bringing down the leaves. They had a journey of about twenty miles ahead of them to reach Sherborne and they planned to spend that night at The Kings Arms at Montacute. The landlord had been in prison with John the Younger, both having been captured after the Battle of Sedgemoor. He had also been one of the few prisoners pardoned by King James. It was not generally known why. Possibly, the King had been flattered by the name of the hostelry, or more likely he had spent a lustful and merry night there sometime in the past.

Young John sat up in the front with his father but Richard, of course, was relegated to sit uncomfortably in the back of the wagon, alongside the bundles of sheep skins that were to be delivered to some dealers in Yeovil and Sherborne. The leather trade - the tanning of skins and hides, and the production of best quality goods, especially gloves - was now really growing in the area.

They travelled along the muddy lanes which were rutted and unmade up. Richard felt quite grumpy. He didn't like being treated as the stupid, younger son. He didn't relish the journey ahead or the prospect of having to go to a new school.

"Bugger this!" he thought and, when neither his father nor brother were looking, he pulled a couple of the fleeces out from their bundles and made a nice comfortable place for himself. They kept him warm too.

The wind increased, and after only having travelled about three miles, a huge gust lifted the wagon sideways. The horses pulled up, snorting and rolling their eyes with fear. Lightning streaked across the sky, and now the rain was lashing at them ferociously.

"We'll have to find shelter or 'twill be the worst for us." shouted John the Younger. "'Tis the William's farm up ahead at Ashill. We'll stop there."

Five minutes later they pulled into the yard of a stone-built, thatched-roofed, farm. Young John jumped down from the wagon and ran to the backdoor and hammered on it. The farmer's wife, rosy-faced Mrs Williams, opened it and welcomed them in.

"Come in all of you!" she cried. "Put your horses and wagon in the barns yonder. Come in out of this terrible weather."

They were soon made comfortable in the stone-flagged kitchen, in front of a huge open hearth that had a bread oven to one side of it. The warmth from the flames of the roaring log fire dried their clothes in no time. Bread, cheese and cider were produced. Mr Williams and his sons joined them for an impromptu meal. There was nothing that could be done outside in such a storm. Anthony Williams and his sons had checked on the coverings to the hayricks in the early morning when it became clear that this was going to be a severe, damaging gale. All the stock had been brought into the barns just in time.

They sat round the huge oak kitchen table, and were served ale and cider by Mary Williams, the Williams's six-year-old daughter. Mary was quite old for her years, an independent and very practical girl, already helping her mother with all the indoor chores. She had bright red, rosy cheeks - obviously a family trait - sparkling chestnut-brown eyes, and very dark, almost black, curly hair. Richard thought he had never seen a prettier girl and fell instantly in love with her.

The grown-ups sat talking round the table long into the afternoon whilst the storm roared around them. Anthony and his wife welcomed the opportunity to catch up on Curry Mallet gossip and were especially interested in what Young John had to say about his 'posh' school. It was intriguing, and somewhat baffling to them, that their neighbours, John Uttermare the Younger and his wife, Anne (née Newman), had made the decision to educate their son in such a way.

Meanwhile, Mary had shyly whispered to Richard, "Come and see what I've got through 'ere in the scullery." He followed her out of the kitchen.

She bent down and picked up two adorable kittens from a withy apple basket lined with a sheepskin. They were about seven weeks old, one black and white, the other tabby. She sat down and stroked them lovingly, whilst they purred away contentedly.

Without knowing what he did, Richard lent over and kissed her very gently on the mouth. He had never kissed a girl before and she had never been kissed like that before. Her large brown eyes flew open, as she looked deeply into his own blue ones. Nothing was said but, even at such a young age, they both knew something momentous had happened.

The storm continued, and the Uttermares were invited by the Williams's to supper and then to stay the night, an invitation they gladly accepted. Next morning the storm had abated, and they left the farm at Ashill at first light.

The journey went well once they had reached the main highway. By nightfall they reached Montacute and stayed at The Kings Arms as planned. Then on again the next day, a short stop in Yeovil to unload the sheepskins, and then the six miles to Sherborne.

Young John was dropped off outside his school. He shook hands with his father and then, going around to the rear of the wagon, he collected his own belongings. He didn't even look at Richard or say 'goodbye'. Without a backward glance, he swaggered through the school gates.

Now it was Richard's turn to be delivered to his fate!

"Come on, down you get lad. Here we are!" cajoled his father who accompanied Richard into the stone building of the newly built Blue School to find the headmaster's quarters. After brief introductions, John the Younger roughly hugged his youngest son, and then left hurriedly.

Richard soon settled into school life and made new friends. They were not like his brother John's classmates - apart from them also all being boys. Many of them were orphans and some were the sons of poor people who were only too happy that their sons would be clothed and fed and given a free education. A lot of the boys had had to fight for their existence up until this point, so they were tough, ill-disciplined, and quick to use their fists. Richard, on the contrary, had had a loving, quiet childhood, so he found it all very difficult.

There was a culture of 'town and gown' in Sherborne. This meant that the boys of the King's School would intimidate and bully, the boys from the Blue School, as they jeeringly called it, whenever they met any of them in the street. They looked down on them and thought of them as guttersnipe.

Saturday was market day in Sherborne, when the boys from both schools were allowed out into the town unsupervised.

There was often trouble between the pupils in and around the market stalls, which was largely ignored by the populace as being just one of those things that happened between boys!

Richard and about five of his friends were enjoying their freedom from the classroom when, suddenly, a mob of about ten bigger, adolescent boys from The King's School, loomed in front of them.

"Now, let's get em!" the biggest roared.

They were very near 'The Conduit'. This was a building that had been used by the Abbey monks for washing. It had become a tradition that 'new boys' from the Blue School would be dunked head-first into the cold water of the Conduit, by the bigger boys of The King's School.

The young boys were grabbed, turned upside down and held under the water. It was actually a very dangerous practise. When his turn came,

The Conduit, Sherborne

John Bucklet 1802, 'The King's School, Sherborne, Dorset
Watercolour on Paper

Richard was terrified and thought he would drown.

Then a voice rang out, "Leave those boys alone!" It came from a slender young woman, dressed in the most fashionable attire of the day. She had a small dog on a lead and was accompanied by her lady's maid. She had a very authoritative manner and, approaching them, reiterated, "Leave those boys alone this instant. I am going to report you to your Headmaster, he is a friend of my father."

She was in fact Elizabeth Collier. Her father was William Collier who had become one of the biggest producers of leather goods in Somerset. He was very rich indeed.

At that moment, who should come alongside her, but none other than Young John Uttermare.

"May I help you Madam?" he asked in an obsequious manner.

As a boy in the upper school, he had some authority over the middle schoolboys. "You heard the lady!" he shouted at them. "Be off with you!"

Letting their captives go free by dumping them unceremoniously onto the ground, the King's School pupils scampered off. The Blue School boys, including Richard, got to their feet, and brushed themselves down, shaking the water out of their hair. John never acknowledged his brother Richard, feigning not to know him. Richard was mortally offended and upset, and as he returned to school with his friends he thought "I really hate him; what an arrogant bastard he is!"

Young John continued walking alongside Ellizabeth Collier and her maid, engaging her in polite society conversation. He found her exceedingly beautiful, with her golden tresses piled high on her head and her slim, corseted bodice accentuating her tiny waist. Her skirts and bodice were of the latest fine brocade, decorated with lace and trimmings. Over this she wore a heavy velvet cape and hood to keep out the cold.

They continued down towards the river. "I often come here," she told him. "Purley Fields next to the riverbank is a wonderful place for Minnie, my little dog to exercise, and one meets such a nice class of person here!"

Indeed, there were many fashionable couples circulating in the short-cropped meadow, many of them with their small dogs, which seemed to be an obligatory add-on to their attire.

Young John and Elizabeth were immediately attracted to one another. She told him when she would next be walking down Cheap Street, and they made a date to meet by the Conduit the following day, after John's lessons had finished.

Their relationship continued until the end of term. John had won a place at Oxford University, and they promised they would write to each other - which they did.

Three years later, John graduated with a first-class honours degree in Latin. Now, however, it was expected that he would return home to run the farm at Curry Mallet with his father. Surprisingly, he agreed to this, but not before he had paid a visit to Elizabeth's father, William Collier, to ask for her hand in marriage. Knowing that the Uttermares were a prosperous farming family who supplied his business with sheep hides, he agreed.

The couple were married in Sherborne Abbey in 1694. It was a huge wedding, paid for by the bride's father. She was his only child. All the Collier's wealthy friends attended, and the Uttermares spruced up for the day and were able to 'keep their end up'.

Young John's descendants, benefitting no doubt from the Colliers inherited wealth, lived the lives of the landed gentry. They mixed with, and married, surgeons, lawyers and Justices of the Peace. Indeed, one became Deputy Lord Lieutenant of Somerset.

As for Richard, he left the Blue School at the age of 16. His father wanted him to join his brother living and working on the farm but the relationship between the two brothers was so frosty that it would never have worked. Richard went to the Williams's farm at Ashill, and asked Anthony Williams if he would employ him as a labourer for bed and board. Williams, a kindly man, readily agreed.

It was no surprise to anyone that Richard and Mary Williams became lovers, and, on 19th April 1704 when Mary was nineteen and Richard was twenty-four, they were married at the Church of St Mary Ashill. Over time Mary gave birth to three daughters - Mary, Anne, and Sarah - and, in 1723, when she was thirty-eight, a son, John, was born.

The descendants of Richard Uttermare all remained as farmers: either as yeomen owning their own land, as tenants of the Duchy of Cornwall, or as labourers working for others. They married farmers' daughters, especially the Meads, and thus increased their holding of land. This branch of the family was influenced for a while, by the rise of Methodism which was sweeping the West Country. As farmers, they were subject to the vagaries of the weather and its harvests. Poverty and even famine stalked the land. Many were forced from the countryside and sought a new and better life in the Colonies, including North America.

One of Richard's great, great grandsons, Thomas William, born 1844 died 1909, was among the many who left the poverty of the Somerset villages to work in the new British Colonies.

Chapter 10 – William Uttermare

Born 1763 died 1842
William, a grandson of Richard, was a tenant farmer in Curry Mallet. Most land to this day in Curry Mallet is owned by the Duchy of Cornwall or, more accurately, by the Prince of Wales. All tenants were, and still are, leaseholders and had to apply to the Court of the Duchy if they wanted to extend their lease, or if they wanted to name their children as leaseholders on their death.

By the time William was a young teenager, Methodism was capturing the attention of everyone. Its charismatic leader, John Wesley, particularly appealed to the lower working classes. This was because he preached that everyone was of equal worth in the eyes of God. He supported the abolition of slavery and spoke out against the terrible prison conditions in Britain. This did not endear him to the ruling classes.

He travelled the countryside on horseback, preaching in the open air to anyone who would listen. He often gathered large crowds around him, becoming something of a celebrity. However, he was not a flamboyant or showy man.

Unlike others of his day, he wore no wig, wearing his straight, shoulder-length hair under a Puritan-style stove pipe hat. Generally, he wore a long, black, woollen coat with a wide white cross-over collar. He was a clean-shaven man with an oval face, aquiline nose and sparkling brown eyes. He had the appearance of a bright-eyed jackdaw.

Between 1743 and 1789, John Wesley preached in Taunton twenty-two times in all, and Methodism grew in popularity in the surrounding Somerset villages, including Curry Mallet. By 1776, when William was just fourteen, his family had become caught up in this fervour.

John Wesley by George Romney (1734-1802)
Oil on Canvas Bequeathed to the National Portrait Gallery, London

Alfred William Hunt (1830-1896) 'John Wesley Preaching from his Father's Tomb'
Oil on Canvas

Many people stopped attending their own local parish churches and, out of their own impoverished pockets, funded the building of chapels and wayside bethels, where they could hear this new style Word of God being preached.

On a cold, early morning in March, William and his parents travelled the short distance to Taunton using the farm wagon. They had heard that John Wesley was due to open the new Octagon Chapel there at midday, and they didn't want to miss it.

When they arrived, they found huge crowds gathered outside the building. They tethered old Bessie, the farm horse, to a tree and joined the throng. Someone kindly let Young William in through the doors of the new chapel, but his parents remained outside in the cold! He found himself sitting beside an old woman who told him, "Do ye know, I've been 'ere since five o' the clock this morning and this place were almost filled then, so ye be lucky to get in, me lad!"

A hush fell over the assembled crowd as John Wesley mounted the pulpit. He taught that it was by 'faith' that a believer became like Christ, and that 'salvation' was not achieved by good works alone. Many were converted, including Young William and his parents.

William married Ann Duke, a farmer's daughter from Isle Abbots, on 1st October 1793. William remained a Methodist and Ann converted to Methodism after their marriage. They had eight children. The eldest, Honour, married a prosperous farmer named Thomas Mead. Their next three children, John, James and Richard, were all baptized in Taunton at the non-conformist Octagon Chapel and Temple as it was now grandly called.

After a while, William decided that he wanted to increase his acreage of land. To do this he had to apply to the Duchy Court.

On the day when his application was due to be considered, he was taken to one side by the court steward who said to him, “Now, I’m afraid you won’t be able to make this application today, unless you drop all this Methodist nonsense. The establishment and the Crown are very jumpy now. They have seen the French Revolution succeed due to the popular uprising of its people, and your Methodism preaches that ‘All are equal in the eyes of God’ which is what these Frenchies call ‘egalité’.

He paused, and then, almost tongue in cheek, added, “as you see I do speak French!”

Then, taking a deep breath and ignoring William’s puzzled look, he raced on, “Also some of your Wesley’s ideas are revolutionary – for instance the abolition of slavery and the reform of prisons and such. The Prince of Wales, George Augustus Frederick, won’t have anyone with such ideas applying for leases on ‘his’ land, so I advise you to go home and think again!”

Feeling somewhat intimidated, William replied, “Well, I thank ye greatly fer yer advice Sir. I shall indeed discuss this with my lady wife.”

Ann agreed that the only way forward was to return to the Anglican fold. “Well, it’s so much more convenient,” she said. “I was getting tired of some of the unkind comments that I sometimes got from some of our neighbours, and we can have the babies baptised there from now on too!”

So it was that, sometime before 1810, William and Ann left the Temple Chapel in Taunton and worshipped from thenceforth at their own parish church of All Saints, in Curry Mallet.

The following year, William presented himself to the Duchy Court, where he was duly admitted and allowed an increased acreage of land.

Sometime later in his life, he again applied to the Court, requesting that five of his now grown-up children, be named as tenants on his Duchy of Cornwall lease upon his death. This request was denied on the grounds that these five had not renounced their Methodism.

Because of this, these five siblings remained poor. They were devout and thought by others to be rather 'odd'. Maybe this was because none of them married or had children and they kept themselves to themselves. Some of them worked as farmers with a few acres of land and others were employed as farm labourers.

By 1861 Ann was living with her brother John, farming four-and-a-half acres, while Elizabeth lived with her brother James, farming fourteen acres. William lodged with some neighbours, the Paul's, working nine acres of farmland.

Sadly, these rather pious, well-meaning, impoverished folk felt forced to give up their Methodism - not only because they were prevented from increasing their leasehold acreage, but because they were being hounded from inside the Methodist Church.

The Methodists organised their churches to run 'band groups'. These were house groups that met during the week. There were to be no more than twelve people in each group. These groups were formed on the lines of men only, women only, or married couples only. They were encouraged to speak about their intimate lives and relationships - to 'share'! They were given permission to gently rebuke each other for any behaviour that they thought was not right.

The five Uttermare children, now in their fifties, had belonged to such groups. They increasingly came in for criticism from fellow members. Finally, one harrowing Sunday at the Temple, they were accused of incest.

Arriving back home, with the girls in tears, William, the eldest of the five proclaimed, "Well I think we've had enough of that. I suggest we all go to the village church from now on."

All Saints Church at Curry Mallet was not happy to baptise adults but the vicar of St James's Church in Taunton - being less traditional and considering himself a modern man - baptised them all together in 1855.

Another of William's and Anne's children was Richard, born 1800 died 1847. He was also baptised as a Methodist, but seemingly was not forced back into the Church of England in the way that his brothers and sisters were. Like them, he was a tenant of very little land.

In 1841 he married Emma Clatworthy, a labourer's daughter. He died after only six years of marriage, leaving Emma a widow, with their three-year-old son Thomas William. She soon remarried. Her new husband was Samuel Humphrey, a prosperous freehold farmer, and she had two more sons with him. Thomas William was brought up as one of the family but remained an Uttermare.

Chapter 11 – Thomas William Uttermare

Born 1844 died 1909
Thomas grew up and worked on his stepfather's farm but, as a stepson, he knew he would receive none of it as an inheritance. That would go to his stepbrothers, the Humphrey boys.

The harvests during the years of his young adult life were poor, with bitterly cold winters lingering into spring. Often the Levels became ice-covered lakes and, in their free time, the children and young people of the village would slide and skate about on them having a wonderful time. Those lucky enough to afford them, wore proper skates.

In 1868, when Thomas was aged twenty-three, the Levels were frozen solid for two months starting from late December onwards. On New Year's Eve the villagers built a huge bonfire on the ice onto which two farm hands manoeuvered a spit. Sam Humphreys provided a suckling pig. This was hung and turned over another smaller brushwood fire. Local musicians with fiddles and drums turned up and people started to dance as night fell.

Everyone knew everyone else, either from school days or from farming. Shopping at the local markets provided the opportunity to meet folk from towns further afield like Yeovil, Bridgwater and Taunton.

Thomas knew all the young people who were there and danced the jigs and waltzes with various girls with whom he had attended the village school. Then he spied Ann Tapp. She had left school a year before him and had gone off to work 'in service' at Lord Digby's estate at Sherborne Castle. Her father was an agricultural machinist, owning a little workshop in Curry Mallet and employing three men and two boys. He was doing well, as agriculture was now becoming increasingly mechanised.

Breathless from the dancing, Thomas sat out the next dance with Ann. Sitting companionably on a straw bale someone had thoughtfully put on the lakeside, they reminisced about their schooldays. Then Ann began to tell Thomas about her job at the castle.

"'Tis up at the crack of dawn I am, lighting all the fires, and then am at the beck and call of Her Ladyship till well after midnight. And that castle is freezing, and we hardly get any time off, and we be paid a pittance," she grumbled. "I shall never get rich this way, that's for sure!" and she laughed mirthlessly.

"Well," replied Thomas, "since we're having a grumble on this fine night, ye know, my life is no better than your'n. I work on that farm from dawn till dusk an we've been having such bad harvests lately, there be no profit in it."

He paused and then added ruefully, "Even if money were to be had, t'would not be coming my way. I've a mind to emigrate to America. I've heard tell there's fertile land to be bought there and it hardly costs a penny. Two of the Mead boys up and went last week. I've a mind to follow them," and, as though he had had a sudden inspiration, he turned, and grasping both her hands in his own said, "Would ye come with me?"

"Is that a proposal?" she giggled shyly. "If so, the answer is yes! Now come on, I can't sit 'ere all night getting frozen to death."

So, it was arranged. They were married in the church at Isle Abbotts late in the spring of 1869 when the thaw came. Ann's father hugged her closely after the ceremony and placed a heavy bag of coins into her hands saying, "We shall all miss ye, but that will help ye fer yer future. I know 'e aint got much," indicating Thomas, "but 'e be a good man, and I know 'e will look after ye. I'll take ye both in the trap meself to the station at Langport tomorrow to see ye off."

Next day, Thomas and Ann, with just a trunk and hand holdalls, were seen off at Langport station by members from both families. They were using the Great Western Railway. First they would travel to Yeovil, then change trains to Salisbury where they would take the London Southwestern Line to Southampton. Steam had revolutionised travel in the last thirty years.

At Southampton they boarded the SS Baltic, a steam ship just arrived from Bremen in Germany, which would take them to New York and thence to a new life. The journey would take about two weeks. This ship was fast. It was a coveted Blue Ribband holder - an award that was given yearly for the fastest steam ship across the Atlantic. It carried two hundred first-class passengers and eighty second-class so was a relatively small vessel for its time. Thomas, being a wise and frugal young man and not knowing what expenses lay ahead, had decided second-class was fine for him and his new wife.

Tired after the long train journey, they headed up the gangplank with the other passengers. Being second-class, they did have a cabin, albeit not as large or as well-equipped as the first-class travellers had.

"You know," Thomas chirpily remarked to Ann, "at least we are not third-class or even stowage class which we might have been on a bigger ship!"

"Well, we must just count our blessings." replied Ann as she sank down, thankfully, onto her quite hard but perfectly clean bunk.

Just then a crew member knocked on the cabin door. "Breakfast is served at seven-thirty, lunch at midday and dinner, for you in second class, is just high tea. All in second-class eat together midships, no mixing with the first-class toffs here!" he joked.

In fact, Ann and Thomas found the food to be very good, a bit like the fare they would have had back home in Curry Mallet. They were not at all bothered that they were not offered the 'Cordon Bleu' menu of the first-class folks.

The Atlantic crossing was uneventful, with calm seas and balmy breezes. The ship entered New York harbour early one morning. All the passengers excitedly lined the rails up on deck as the SS Baltic steamed regally along the shores of The Battery, the southernmost point on the Manhattan peninsular. The ship berthed alongside the Immigration Centre called Castle Garden. As there were only first- and second-class passengers on the Baltic, they were saved the ignominious checks that third-class and stowage passengers had to endure in later times at the Ellis Island Immigration Centre.

Thomas and Ann showed their immigration papers and were waved politely on, with just a gentle caution from the officials that they should be aware of thieves and con merchants who were around, ready to lead newcomers astray. William and Ann thanked them, and then called to one of the many porters to manage their baggage. They were soon out into the noise and bustle of streets of Lower Manhattan, New York.

Thomas knew where they were headed. He had heard the Mead brothers talking about the fertile farmland that one could buy cheaply in Illinois, near Chicago, on the Great Lakes. Bundling their belongings into a steam-powered tram which terminated at Grand Central Station, they sank down thankfully into two unoccupied seats.

"Well, we've made it. What an adventure!" breathed Ann, looking out of the window. She had never been further in her life than Sherborne, and the tall buildings and scurrying people of all nationalities were something to behold.

The journey by railroad from New York to the little town of Joliet took all day. Once there, they looked around and found lodgings. Thomas made enquiries and heard of one hundred and forty acres of prime pasture for sale, just outside the town. The land here was flat, but rich and alluvial, probably brought down in ages past by the Mississippi River which still flowed nearby.

There was just a wooden cabin on this land, but it would do for now. A well outside produced sparkling, clear water, and a small spinney nearby would provide them with wood to burn for warmth and for cooking.

Over the years, and indeed within their lifetime, Thomas and Ann built a fine-looking farmstead with wooden clapboard walls and a tiled roof. They raised cattle on the rich pasture, as had their forebears in Somerset, and planted apple orchards - also reminiscent of home. They grew wheat, oats and barley on the flat, open land which year after year produced an abundant harvest for them. They became well-respected members of the community and pillars of the local Episcopal church.

Ann had been aged twenty-five when they arrived in America and she didn't give birth to her first child, Winifred Robinett, until she was thirty years old. Her second baby, also a girl, Sarah, or Sadie as she was known, was born when Ann was forty-six.

One morning in 1908 Thomas said to Ann, "You know it's my sixty-fourth birthday this year and I've a yen to see the 'Old Country' once more before I shuffle off this mortal coil!"

"Well, I want to come too!" chimed in Winifred, who was now aged twenty-four and wanted to see a bit more of the world. Thomas knew he would value his elder daughter's company on the long journey. It was agreed that Winifred, having the neatest handwriting in the family, would write to Thomas Mead Uttermare and ask him if it would be possible for her and her father to come and stay with him for a while. He was their closest, living male relative. He was a bachelor living at and running Bowdens Farm at Curry Rivel.

Thomas had replied quite quickly and said 'of course' he would be delighted to welcome both to his farm. He explained that his elderly father Richard had now retired and was living with his daughter, Marion, and her husband, Frank, on their farm in Langport. Winifred replied that she and her father looked forward to meeting him and other members of the Uttermare and Tapp families in the spring. They left Sadie and Ann in charge of the farm and took the two-funneled steam ship, RMS Oceanic II, from New York to Southampton.

They arrived in late May 1908. They travelled by train from the port and, after a wearisome journey, arrived at Langport station. Outside, they found horses and carriages, ready and waiting to take passengers to their destinations.

"Can you take us to Bowdens Farm, Hambridge, Curry Rivel please?" Winifred asked of a stout, red-faced driver.

"Hop in Miss," he said with a cheeky grin as he helped get Thomas and all their baggage into a rather rickety old carriage.

Bowdens Farm turned out to be a commodious farmhouse with a detached dairy house, and a walled kitchen and fruit garden. It also had its own homestead or home farm called Wiltown. This had probably been built in the mid-seventeenth century, but Bowdens Farm was added later. Winifred thought that it might have been built at the turn of the nineteenth century. It certainly looked very prosperous with its red brick walls and tiled roof.

Thomas Mead Uttermare welcomed them gruffly. He was thirty-nine years old and now lived alone in the big house with his housekeeper, Mrs. Lois Hooper and one house maid, Betsy.

Winifred thought he had the appearance of a man living without a wife, in other words, lacking someone to make sure he had on a clean shirt when

RMS Oceanic II 1899-1914
Artificially Coloured Postcard

Bowdens Farm where Richard and Honour lived between 1891 and 1901 shown here with their youngest daughters, Bessie and Frances Louise

he welcomed guests, which he hadn't! However, he had very obviously flattened down his unruly hair with warm water and a comb for the occasion. Winifred felt that this gave him a sort of vulnerability.

Betsy showed them to their rooms which were furnished in the heavy Victorian manner but proved to be comfortable enough. "There's a cold supper for ye in the dining room and Mr. Thomas will join ye there," and she curtsied in an old-fashioned way which Winifred found charming. Servants had long since given up such traditions in America.

At supper the conversation was rather stilted. It was obvious that Thomas was accustomed to just his own company and the travellers were tired after their long journey, but Winifred did her best at small talk. However, one thing he did tell them was that his sister, Elizabeth Alice Taylor, who lived in Taunton, would be visiting them the next day with 'all her tribe' as he put it.

The following morning, sure enough, a large wagon, pulled by two beautiful grey horses, clattered into the yard. As soon as it was stationary, three children - two girls, one about fifteen, and the other about twelve, and a little boy - tumbled out, all fighting to be the first in through the front door to see Uncle Tom.

The girls were dressed in high-necked, heavy white cotton pinafore dresses, frilled at the cuffs, and they wore black leather ankle boots. The young boy wore a bright blue jacket with large buttons down the front and a large white cotton collar edged with lace. His little legs were clad in voluminous, bell-bottomed, sailor-style trousers.

The children's mother, Elizabeth Alice, followed more sedately. She was a tiny, middle-aged woman, dressed in the Edwardian style of the day. Her ample bosom was covered by a beautiful pleated and frilled silk blouse and, around her neck, hung a heavy gold necklace with a large gold pendant. The wide sleeves of her blouse were frilled to the elbow.

Her cream linen floor-length skirt was full, but she was without the stays and bustle that her mother, Honour, would have worn.

For the middle and upper classes, this was an altogether carefree age, and this was a free-spirited family, who loved singing, drawing, swimming, picnicking and travelling abroad for holidays in the Alps and Ireland. Being wealthy allowed them to indulge in these hobbies and interests.

The head of the family was Theophilus Taylor who owned a glove factory in Taunton. There were six children in all, but today the two older boys had been left at home with the eldest daughter, Florence. They lived at Rosalind Villa - a spacious Victorian residence situated in a leafy part of the town.

The three children - Alice May, fifteen; Nora, twelve; and young George - had pounced on their beloved Uncle Tom. He adored them, and his usual gruffness, which was just shyness, was completely forgotten as they playfully wrestled with him on the drawing room carpet.

"Now stop all that at once," called their mother crisply. "Get up and greet your American relations properly," she added, as Thomas William and Winifred appeared in the doorway.

Introductions were made and lunch was served in the dining room by Betsy and Mrs. Lois Hooper, the housekeeper. This was an altogether livelier meal than the one of the previous evening. Elizabeth Alice was a great conversationalist, and the children were also allowed at table, which made the atmosphere informal and relaxed.

The conversation shifted to a discussion about how Thomas William and Winifred were related to the others seated there. Elizabeth Alice had a very good idea of the family tree, and being a competent artist, drawing

Standing left to right Nora, Harold, Florence, Bernard and Alice May
Seated Theophilus Taylor, George Taylor, Elizabeth Alice Taylor
Photo taken about 1906

Photo of Taylors on holiday in the Alps

Left to Right: Miss Dudman (from Worcester), Theophilus, Elizabeth Alice.
Gap of Dunloe, County Kerry, 1913

out pencil and paper from her handbag, deftly drew it out for them. Then she warned them with a twinkle in her eye, "You do realise that we are from the 'poor' side of the family. There is another branch of the Uttermares who are the 'posh' folk. You see there was some kind of dispute many years ago between two brothers - a John and a Richard I believe," and her voice trailed off as though she was trying to remember all she had read and heard about her mother's and her father's family – both of whom shared the same great grandparents.

Then, coming out of her reverie, she continued. "I can take you and show you the plaques in the church at Hatch Beauchamp, very near here. I recall seeing there a plaque with three names on it."

"If I remember correctly, the top name is for a John Uttermare who purchased the Lordship of the Manor of Hatch Beauchamp in 1722. Now this means that he only bought the title, not the Manor House itself which is a rather ugly Palladian-style mansion. He lived at Hatch Green Farm and he farmed the large acreage there. I think he might have been a somewhat arrogant man as he liked to use the title of Lord. He passed this title down to his son James, from whence it passed down to his grandson, John.

"I know it's confusing but, as we are all staying here tonight, why don't we have a jaunt out to Hatch Beauchamp tomorrow to visit the church and then you will be able to see the plaques for yourselves."

Of course, the 'Americans' were thrilled at the prospect and so Mrs. Hooper was summoned and asked to prepare a picnic lunch for the following day.

The day dawned with a misty haze above the Levels, presaging the heat to come. The family and their American relations set off after a hearty breakfast. Uncle Tom stayed home as he had far too much to attend to on the farm and family history didn't interest him. Frankly, he couldn't understand the fascination!

The horses pulled up at the wooden, elaborately carved lychgate of Hatch Beauchamp Church. The children scampered off into the church yard and began a game of hide-and-seek around the gravestones. The stooped figure of an elderly man slowly emerged from behind the church. He scowled at the children and then, seeing the rather grand wagon and immaculate grey horses and the three finely dressed adults walking up the gravel path, decided against reprimanding them.

Seeing him, Elizabeth Alice, wearing her most disarming smile, introduced herself and her two companions. Doffing his cap the man bowed slightly, and said "Pleased to meet you, Ma'am. I be Paul Coates, church warden and grave digger 'ere abouts."

Elizabeth Alice explained that they had come to look at the Uttermare family plaques.

Paul Coates led the way, pushing open the heavy oak church door and ushering them in. The plaques were above the doorway and easy to read.

Winifred was busily noting down the family details from the plaques when Paul Coates, who had been hovering in the background, came forward and said, "You know t'wer a bit o' scandal with thick family. Some stories were passed down in my family, who 'av been church wardens 'ere fer generations. Would ye like me to tell ye about it?"

"Bet yer bottom dollar we would." answered Winifred, almost skipping with excitement. But Elizabeth Alice looked somewhat apprehensive, wondering what might be coming next!

Encouraged, Paul Coates continued, "The tale is that John, that you see at the top of the plaque, had a brother called Robert. John's daughter Anne were obliged to marry Robert's son William to keep land and property in the family. T'was known as an 'intermarriage' fer they were first cousins."

"T'was John, at top of the plaque, who bought the title of Lordship of the Manor of Hatch Beauchamp and he passed it down, first to his son James, yer see it there, and thence it went to his grandson, John, at the bottom there," he pointed with a gnarled, old, shaking index finger.

"But that's not all," he chuckled. "That last John had a brother, William, and they didn't get on by all accounts. Talk was they shared a mistress called Ann Gamlin. She were at various times both servant and mistress to both of them."

"First, she lived with and worked for one brother, and then she moved house, and lived with t'other one. She had a little girl called Mary-Ann who was generally known to be William's daughter, but I don't know if he ever acknowledged her. She wer known hereabouts as Mary-Ann Gamlin. William later had another servant, Elizabeth Morrish, an 'e ad a child with 'er too. 'E were called Edward Morrish. So, you see this William, he had children out of wedlock with 'is servants. But I fear I have said enough."

"Well, yes I think you have!" replied Elizabeth Alice tartly and, turning to Thomas and Winifred, said, "Let's gather up the children and go for that picnic. There's a pretty spot that I know in the Quantocks called Halford Glen which you will love. Come on!"

Thomas William and Winifred spent a truly memorable summer holiday down on the Levels visiting the Tapps and the Uttermares. They returned to New York on 11th November 1908, once again on board the two-funneled steam ship, RMS Oceanic II. That same year, Thomas William Uttermare received his naturalisation papers and became a citizen of the United States of America.

Chapter 12 - Winifred Robinett Uttermare

Born 1884 died 31st March 1939

Once back home on the farm in Joliet, Illinois, Winifred could not settle. It was just a small farming community and she had enjoyed - and now missed - the more sophisticated and cultured way of life that she had found in Taunton with her 'English' family. The farm was now being run by her sister Sadie and her husband Daniel Cockle. Winifred and Sarah's parents had both died in 1909.

Winifred remained a spinster and, in 1911, feeling that there was nothing for her at home, she planned once more to embark - this time alone - on the long journey back to the little village of Isle Abbotts on the Somerset Levels. This was where her parents had lived in their youth and where many of her mother's family, the Tapps, now resided. Her Uncle and Aunt, Joshua and Mary Crocker, had answered the letter that she had sent to them, saying that she would be very welcome to stay with them at their home, 'The Laurels'.

Winifred was a member of the Joliet Episcopal Church and attended every Sunday, as did the rest of the family. This church was a Protestant one and was really an offshoot of the Church of England back in Britain.

One Sunday, a newly ordained young minister arrived. His name was Pierre Bourdin and his family was French. Winifred was captivated by his sermon, as much by its well-researched and original content, as by his attractive French accent.

After the service, he bade farewell to his congregation at the church door. Winifred shook hands with him, and he asked if he could visit her and the rest of her family at the farm. He emphasized that pastoral care was very important to him.

He duly arrived one sunny afternoon and Saidie and Winifred spent a lovely time drinking tea and enjoying Somerset scones with him. Saidie had to leave after a while to help her husband with the milking.

Pierre and Winifred continued chatting, and Winifred told him of her desire to spread her wings and revisit Somerset. Pierre said that he wanted to go to France, as he had never been there, and that he had many relatives in Normandy whom he had never met. Pierre suggested they make the journey together, as she would need a chaperone for such a long and hazardous journey. Winifred loved the idea, and Saidie and her husband thought it a very sensible arrangement.

The two set off, firstly taking the steam train, and then crossing the Great Lakes by paddle steamer. Finally, they arrived in Montreal, which seemed like a huge metropolis to both of them. They found lodgings for the night at a respectable hotel. This was French-speaking Canada, so Pierre was a very useful person to have for a companion as Winifred spoke no French at all.

The following morning, they made their way down to the bustling port. They queued in line at a rough wooden kiosk to buy their tickets. In the queue immediately ahead, was a tall, well-built man, in his thirties, who quickly fell into conversation with them. He seemed very keen to tell them all about himself and his life history. It appeared he was a travelling dentist on his way to England, where he said people would pay good money to cure their toothaches. His name was Charles Hudson, an American citizen like themselves, and he told them that he was married with two young sons. He mentioned that this was not the first time that he had made this ‘business trip’ and that it was great fun aboard. All sorts of things went on once well out to sea!

Having purchased their tickets for the RMS Victorian and presented their passports, the three walked up the gangplank together and were shown to their individual second-class cabins.

Charles was right, and to Winifred's delight, life on board did turn out to be fun. There were a lot of other young people on the ship, some of them, like Winifred and Pierre, were travelling back to their country of origin from whence their parents had fled a generation earlier.

A young woman called Lucy Kelly, whose Irish family originally came from Belfast, often joined Charles, Winifred and Pierre for the evenings, making a very jolly foursome for meals in the salon as well as partaking in dancing and singing. As to the card games, they were played all over the ship, night and day.

On the final evening of their voyage, after a special 'last night' meal with wine in the salon, Charles suggested that the four friends should spend the evening, as they had often done, playing cards. They had taken it in turns to 'host' their games in one or other of their cabins. Winifred thought it was her turn, and merrily invited them all along.

Charles bought along a bottle of red wine, and they settled down to a very convivial evening - their laughter growing louder and their game of gin-rummy going rapidly downhill.

As midnight approached, Lucy reminded them all that they would need to be up in good time the next day as they needed to pack up their belongings and get a good position on deck if they wanted to catch a first glimpse of the port and the city of Liverpool.

Pierre and Lucy got up from the card table, bidding goodnight to Winifred, but Charles said he would stay for a few moments and help Winifred tidy up the cards and wine glasses.

As soon as the cabin door swung closed behind Pierre and Lucy, Charles surprised Winifred by gently encircling her waist with his arms as she straightened up from her chair. Then he kissed her passionately. She had drunk far more wine that evening than she had intended, and she found herself responding to his advances. Taking her by the hand, he began to lead her over to the bunk next to the wall. All at once the alcoholic haze lifted and she came to her senses. Remembering that he was a married man with two young sons, she was horrified at what she might be about to do. She gently pulled away from him and he relinquished her hand with a sigh of disappointment. Silently, he kissed her again, but this time chastely on the cheek, and then he left.

Leaning against the inside of the closed door, Winifred's first feeling was one of relief. Who knew what might have happened if she had allowed herself to be carried away in the moment? She got to thinking about the choices one made in life. What happened if one took the left turn or the right turn? If one married one man or a different one? Or was one's life all mapped out even before one was born as some folk in her church believed?

Then, giving herself a little shake, she said to herself that these were mighty big questions, and ones that philosophers far brighter than herself had asked for centuries. She realized that tomorrow, she could ask Pierre what he thought about these things. He was such a thoughtful and well-read young man, and she was sure he would have an answer for her.

Next morning there was no sign of either Charles or Lucy amongst the milling throng of passengers who had got up early to sight landfall and to be first off the ship.

Winifred and Pierre leaned companionably, but silently, together against the guardrail of the deck. Then, completely out of the blue it seemed to him, Winifred asked Pierre her questions from the night before.

Looking thoughtfully at her, he solemnly told her that, in this life, there would be many questions to which the answer is never known but that, in the next life, all would be made clear - and he quoted St Paul in his letter to the Corinthians, to her.

She thanked him for his answer and the two of them disembarked the RMS Victorian and went their separate ways. Throughout her life, and especially when she knew it was drawing to a close, Winifred often pondered these wise words and drew much comfort from them.

Once back in Somerset, and living at 'The Laurels' in Isle Abbots, she found herself often thinking about, and being intrigued by, family history. She shared this passion with Elizabeth Alice Taylor, who would often invite her to Rosalind Villa in Taunton to spend time there with the family.

Elizabeth Alice was only too delighted when it seemed that a special friendship was developing between her son, Harold, and Winifred.

The Taylor family photographed outside Rosalind Villa, Richmond Road, Taunton Elizabeth Alice with Alice May on her knee, Theophilus holding Harold's hand, Bernard sitting on the grass, and Florence standing.

Harold, born in 1890, was the Taylor's elder son. He was twenty-one when Winifred met up with him again in 1911. He was a good-looking young man with kind blue eyes, an aquiline nose, neat ears, and a generous mouth - all set in the oval-to-heart-shaped face that was characteristic of all the Taylors.

He was fun to be with, and often made Winifred laugh with his quick, clever wit. He loved the outdoors, as did she, and enjoyed swimming and playing cricket for the local Taunton side. He also loved drawing and singing and appreciated a well-written detective novel.

He had left Taunton School with good grades and became an articled clerk to a firm of auctioneers. He had attested for the West Somerset Yeomanry and spent some summer evenings practising drills with them.

Neither he nor Winifred nor, indeed, any of the rest of the family had any idea of the horrors of the 'Great War' which were to come. These were 'Halcyon Days' at the end of the peaceful and gentle Edwardian era.

Winifred was very much taken under the wing of this family, and she was often with them for weekends or during the holidays, such as Christmas or Easter. She always sat next to Harold at mealtimes, when all the family ate together at the huge mahogany table in the dining room at Rosalind Villa.

It was at one such Easter Sunday lunchtime that Winifred heard for the first time about how Harold's sister, Alice May, known to all the family as May, was now being hailed as a heroine in the local press.

"Haven't you heard?" asked Harold of Winifred. "Young May here, is the talk of the town."

"Well, do tell," replied Winifred, all agog.

"I think May should tell the story," said their father Theo, who was sitting at the head of the table. "It's her story after all."

May coloured a bit but was more than eager to tell her side of it.

"Well, you know, now I've left school, I help Father out at the factory. I help in the office with the accounts and such like and am getting to know how the glove factory business works.

"One morning, I was looking out of the office window which overlooks the River Tone, French Weir, and the meadows beyond. I was thinking how pretty it all looked, when I noticed a young woman walking up and down, along the towpath. She seemed to be very agitated, muttering to herself, and her face was distorted, with tears rolling down her cheeks. The more I watched, the more worried I became. I called to Mr. Jell, the head clerk, and pointed out to him what was happening."

"I agree with you, she does look very distressed," he said. "Come with me, let's see if we can help."

"We dashed downstairs and outside," she continued, "but it was too late. By the time we got to the spot, the young woman had thrown herself in the river. The current was running quite fast, and she was being taken rapidly down towards the weir. She was thrashing her arms around and, from time-to-time, she completely disappeared under the water.

Mr. Jell and I ran along the path keeping up with her as best we could. Then Mr. Jell suddenly stopped, pulled off his shoes, and jumped in after her. He was a strong swimmer and managed to catch hold of her clothing, but she was thrashing around, and after a few seconds he lost his grip on her, and she screamed and disappeared."

May paused for breath and then continued.

“Well, I had to do something and, as you know we are all good swimmers in this family. Indeed, father taught each of us how to swim in the river, and recently, Harold, with his army training, has taught me life-saving techniques. So, I tugged off my shoes, tucked my skirt into my bloomers, and jumped in too.

“I quickly caught up with the girl who, thankfully, had now resurfaced, and I managed to pull both her shoulders backwards so that she was facing upwards. I cupped her chin in my left hand and pulled her chin up clear out of the water as I had, thankfully, been taught to do. But now this was for real, and it had to work! I told her to rest her head in the crook of my neck, to stop panicking, and to just trust me, and that all would be well. Do you know, she did just that - must be something to do with my calming influence on people!” May joked. Then she continued.

“I managed to get us both to the bank where there were some overhanging tree branches, and I clutched one with my right hand. Some people had heard the commotion, and they hauled us both up the bank and onto the towpath. These kind people put their coats around us, and then Mr Jell appeared, dripping water everywhere and looking a bit sheepish. The girl was shivering like a leaf, and just kept saying ‘Sorry! Sorry! Sorry!’ as she choked back her tears. We made our way back to the factory where Papa put me and the girl - who I now knew to be called Dolly - into a cab and sent us straight back home. Mr. Jell was given the rest of the day off!

“When we got back here Mama made us both have hot baths and put us to bed! Dolly slept for hours, but I was far too excited to sleep. When Dolly eventually woke up, Mama gave her some hot cocoa to drink, and Dolly told us the whole story.

“It turns out, that Dolly’s father, who works in our factory, regularly gets drunk, and beats her and her mother when he has been drinking. She and her mother are both outworkers, gloving for us. They often do not have money for food or rent because her father squanders it on drink.

HEROIC RESCUES AT TAUNTON.

THREE LIVES ENDANGERED IN FLOODED RIVER.

The present age is crowded with heroic acts on the part of our soldiers at the various fronts, but heroism at home is still displayed by those who for one reason or another are unable to serve their country in the fighting line, as was evidenced at Roughmoor Fields, Taunton, on Friday last, when two persons almost lost their life in an endeavour to save a young lady from drowning in a flooded river. Fortunately all the parties were brought safely to land, and to-day are little the worse for their terrible experience.

It appears that on Friday morning last the employees at Messrs. Taylor's glove factory at Richmond-road, which overlooks the Roughmoor Fields through which the River Tone runs, noticed a young woman behaving in a rather extraordinary manner. The morning was somewhat boisterous and she was walking aimlessly up and down the fields without hat or coat. At first it was thought she was a "weather crank" or some person out for the benefit of her complexion, but from her later movements it was evident that something unusual was happening. Closer investigation revealed the fact that the young lady was walking up and down the towing path for a given distance, and that she wiped the mud from her boots in a clean white pinafore. Moreover, she endeavoured to avoid all passers by, and seemed to be in a general nervous condition. Mr. Theo. Taylor's attention was drawn to this extraordinary occurrence, and he immediately requested his daughter, Miss May Taylor, and Miss Shillson, who is also employed at the factory, to go to the girl in a friendly way and endeavour to induce her to go to his home. Miss Taylor and Miss Shillson, accompanied by Mr. Oaksford another employee set out across the fields to seek the girl, and on their way saw Mr. Jeil, of Richmond-road, who also accompanied them. Whilst going to the girl they noticed that she did not turn in the usual place but continued her walk along the river bank, and accordingly Mr. Oaksford struck off across the field to intercept her, the others following the girl as fast as the strong wind which was blowing would allow them to go. It was apparent to them that the girl's mind was a blank, and when she got to the Norton Brook she threw up her pinafore and was lost from view. Mr. Oaksford however, was able to see what had occurred and his shouts caused Mr. Jeil to run forward, and he then saw the girl floating down the river. Following the heavy wind and rain the river was much swollen and practically in flood, but, without a moment's hesitation, Mr. Jeil jumped into the river to rescue the girl. Miss Taylor and Miss Shillson had hastened to the scene, and immediately they heard Mr Jeil shout "Help, come on, I shall go if you don't come on!" Miss Taylor, seeing the plight of the two people in the river, immediately plunged in, but found that the current was beyond her strength and she was also placed in difficulties. She tried to get behind Mr. Jeil and the girl to render assistance but was unable to reach them, and had to hold on to the branch of a tree. Meanwhile Mr. Jeil had also got the girl to a tree, and rescurer and rescued clung on to the branches. Mr. Oaksford had by this time reached the river, and assisted all three from their precarious positions.

On being taken from the water the girl was successfully treated, and heartily thanked her rescuers for their gallant action. Miss Taylor and Miss Shillson made the unfortunate girl as comfortable as possible, and Mr. Oaksford lent her his coat, and she was then taken to Mr. Taylor's house. Meanwhile, Miss Taylor, whose clothes were wet through on account of her being in the water for nearly ten minutes, ran on to advise her mother, and [illegible] to [illegible] warmth for herself, and upon the girl's arrival she was given a hot bath and put to bed and in the evening was taken back to her friends.

"To cap it all, Dolly's fiancé has joined the Royal Navy, and she doesn't know when, or if, she will see him again. She told us that he was recruited by agents working for the navy, who had recently come to Taunton. Apparently, the Navy needs young recruits to man the new steam warships that Admiral Lord Fisher, First Sea Lord, has ordered to be built to combat the threat from the German Navy. They promised that they would pay recruits more than if they stayed working in the glove factory or on nearby farms."

May took a deep breath and said, "So that's my story, and it's going to be in the Taunton Gazette next week. A young reporter came to the house yesterday, interviewed me, and wrote it all down."

All the family had listened intently to May's account, and her father, who was looking very serious, slowly said, "I will have a quiet word with Dolly's father, it sounds like he needs some help with his drinking problem. I have some friends in the Temperance Movement who I am sure could give the whole family some support."

Harold chipped in, "Maybe we should be thinking about increasing the wages of our workers." Looking meaningfully at his father he added, "You know there really is a huge difference between their incomes and what we earn from the glove factory."

The meal over, the family went its separate ways.

Winifred and Harold cycled up into the Quantock Hills for the afternoon. Stopping, they left their bikes propped up against oak trees growing in the leafy shade of Halford Glen. Then, following the stream up between the valley sides, they emerged onto the top of the bracken-covered hillside.

"Let's sit down awhile," Harold suggested. "You know," he gently said to Winifred, "I fear that what that young woman, Dolly, said to Mama and May about local young men being recruited into the Royal Navy, is right. I have read in the newspapers that the Germans are 'sabre rattling' and war may be on the horizon." Winifred's face clouded over, and Harold instantly felt sorry for spoiling the lovely spring afternoon.

Without thinking, he bent over and kissed her. She instantly and eagerly responded to him, kissing him back with passion. He was the first man that she had ever felt attracted to. Even though she had travelled by boat to England on two occasions, the second time on her own with Pierre as a nominal chaperone, and had met all kinds of men during that time, none were like Harold. She knew that many folks, especially her family back home, regarded her as a confirmed spinster.

Later, gently pulling away from each other, they got to their feet, brushing the dry grass and bracken off their clothes.

Winifred and Harold continued with this loving friendship. Despite their age difference - he being six years her junior - they had an understanding, and most probably would have married. But, just as Harold had feared, on 28th July 1914 the Great War began, shattering all their lives.

Harold had by that time joined the Royal Wiltshire Yeomanry Regiment serving as a Corporal in 'B' squadron of the unit. When war broke out, he was sent to fight in Salonica, Greece.

Salonica, or Thessaloniki as it was also known, was a large town situated on the Northen Coast of Greece. The Allies, at this time, comprised the British, Russians, French, Serbians, and soldiers from the British Commonwealth. The enemy were the Germans, the Turks and the Bulgarians.

The Bulgarians had invaded Serbia, and the British and their Allies were sent to prevent its demise. However, the British arrived too late, and Serbia fell. The best the British and their Allies could do was to create a huge entrenchment and barracks on the outskirts of Salonica town, with the Aegean Sea behind them and the Rhodope mountain range in front of them. The latter formed the frontier between Bulgaria and Greece. From these barracks, the Allies would leave with all their equipment and armoury to fight the Bulgarians - or Bulgars as the British liked to call them - who would come over the mountains to engage in mortal combat.

It was feared at this moment that King Constantine of Greece was sympathetic to the Germans, although his Prime Minister supported the British. This meant that Greece could not be relied upon to stand firm against the enemy. If Greece fell too, the Bulgarians would sweep eastward heading towards the Gallipoli Peninsular, which was another theatre of the Great War. Here, the Turks were manning the heights above the Dardanelles Straights. The British and their allies were striving to take the Straights and also Istanbul, and continue via the Bosporus into The Black Sea, in order to fight off the Turks, who were attacking the Russians in Odessa.

It was all very complicated, and in the end turned out to be a failed mission with a huge loss of life.

So it was that Harold Taylor arrived at the Allied Barracks in late August 1914 having been ferried ashore by landing craft from bigger ships moored in the Aegean. Conditions were rough and makeshift and the food understandably poor.

The aim of this campaign was to push back the 'Bulgars', preventing them from coming down from the mountain range and into Greece.

Harold and his regiment were sent out regularly from the barracks to engage the enemy. They were armed with rifles and bayonets and the fighting could be hand-to-hand and very frightening and bloody.

Autumn came, and then, in November, the snow fell and in places was up to the men's shoulders making patrols slow and clumsy. There was frost at night with temperatures well below zero, and the soldier's greatcoats would crack, rendering them useless. In the daytime, fog rolling down from the mountain tops, would completely reduce visibility and block out any feeble rays of sun. It was indeed, thought Harold, 'miserable'.

On one such day, he and his patrol heard voices coming through the dense mist ahead. Then shots were fired at them and, although it had been random fire, six of the men were hit and lay bloodied in the snow. The men of the Royal Wiltshire Yeomanry returned fire, heard groans and screams but never saw their enemy, who fled like phantoms.

Harold's 'B' squadron was so depleted by this attack that, once back at the barracks in Salonica, he and the remains of his regiment were transferred to the Surrey Yeomanry. At the end of 1916, he was promoted to the rank of 2nd Lieutenant, where he was part of the Machine Gun Corps.

Meanwhile, in the village of Isle Abbotts nothing really changed. Winifred lived with her aunt and uncle, Joshua and Mary Crocker, at 'The Laurels' and next door in 'Colliers' lived her mother's brother, Robert Tapp and his wife, Elizabeth, with their son Samuel, aged thirty-nine and their daughter Sarah.

Like the Taylors, the Tapps had shown kindness and hospitality to Winifred and she was often invited to Sunday lunch with them after the morning service at the Baptist Chapel. It had become obvious to Winifred, aged thirty, that Mrs Tapp, her aunt, saw her as an excellent match for her bachelor son. The fact that they were first cousins was of no consequence to her.

Some young unattached men did volunteer to join the army as soon as war was declared. Possibly Mrs Tapp was fearful that her 'dear son' would do the same. She dropped hints into Samuel's ear and one Sunday, after lunch, he asked Winifred to come and admire the tomatoes he had successfully grown in the garden.

She was so surprised when he said with no preamble whatsoever, "Winnie, will you marry me?"

"Well, I will think about it," she replied, and she did.

She really loved Harold, but he was now in Salonica and he had never truly committed himself to her. She knew conditions out there were terrible and, although his letters to her were chirpy enough, they certainly were not romantic, but then neither was Samuel who was busy tying up

Alice May

Nora Taylor sister of Alice May
with her mother, Elizabeth Alice

Standing Left to Right: George, Harold, Hilda, Bernard, Nora, Archie Howard
Seated Left to Right: Alice May, Theophilus, Elizabeth Alice, Florence

his tomatoes! And she wasn't getting any younger! And she loved Somerset!

"Yes," she said, "I will marry you."

They were married on 2nd September 1914 at the Baptist Chapel in Isle Abbotts by the Reverend J.S. Scofield and, of course, Mrs. Tapp was delighted!

It was not long after that, that the posters bearing the words, 'Your Country Needs YOU' with the pointing finger, arrived everywhere in the village. Now all the men felt obliged to join up. Samuel joined the Seaforth Highlanders and, in August 1916, he too was sent to fight in Salonica.

So it was, that both Harold Taylor and Samuel Tapp, were fighting in the same theatre of war in Northern Greece.

Samuel had been trained as a medical orderly and stretcher bearer. Occasionally he drove the rickety ambulances that the army had shipped out from England.

He was kept very busy ferrying casualties back from the front to the 31st Clearing Station, Salonica. This was the medical facility in which the moderately seriously wounded would receive treatment from doctors, nurses and surgeons.

For the following six months, Samuel worked in terrible conditions, picking up the dead and injured from the battlefields and dugouts in the rocky, barren mountain terrain. Then, in March, there was a huge incursion of Bulgars. Losses on both sides were massive.

Arriving at a machine gun post situated on rising ground overlooking a valley, Sam could see bodies strewn everywhere. Some were immobile, others still alive. This post had been overrun by the enemy who, for whatever reason, had moved on.

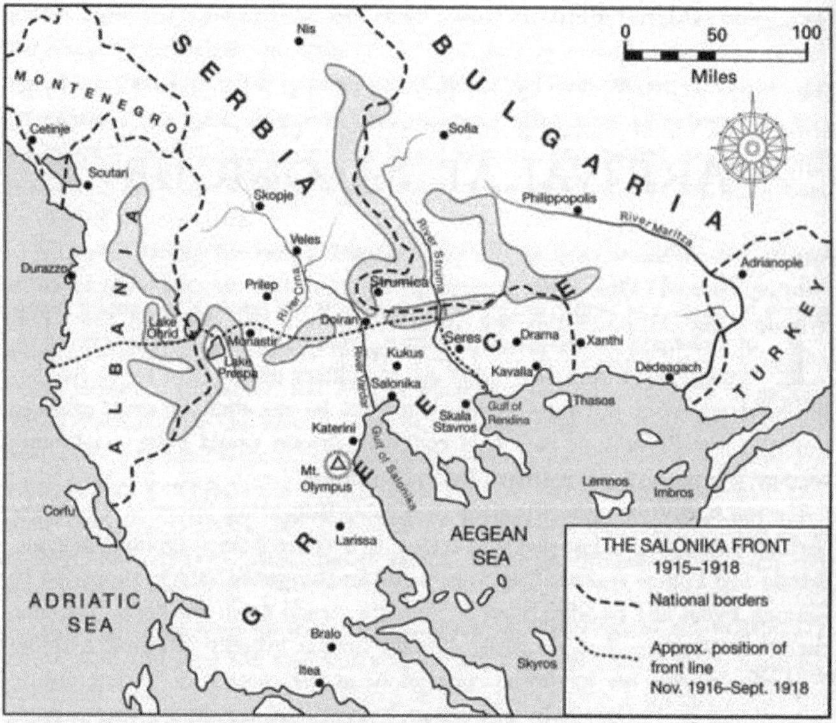

The Salonika front, 1915-1918, URL: https://nzhistory.govt.nz/media/photo/salonika-front-19151918, (Manatū Taonga — Ministry for Culture and Heritage), updated 30-Jul-2014

Sam and his comrades picked up and carried four of the injured men into their ambulance on a stretcher. They knew there were other ambulances following on behind who would pick up the rest of the casualties and the fallen.

Sam soon got to work tending the leg and head wounds of one of the patients. This man was a junior officer and seemed in a lot of pain. He kept falling in and out of consciousness. Sam knew it was vital to keep him awake.

"What's your name, Sir?" he asked gently.

"Lieutenant Harold Taylor, Surrey Yeomanry," came the groggy reply. The man had a slight Somerset 'burr' which Sam immediately recognised as a Taunton one. He was good at spotting the differences between a Bridgwater, a Curry Rival, or even a Yeovil accent. His own was pure Somerset Levels and very broad.

"Do ye hail from Taunton and are ye related to the Taylors who have the glove factory in the middle of town?"

"Yes indeed," replied Harold. "My father Theophilus owns the factory."

"Well, I'll be blowed! My wife Winifred is related to the Taylors and she used to spend a lot of time with the family. Does her name mean anything to you? Were you ever friendly with her?"

Sleepily, Harold replied, "Well, yes it does and we were more than that too for a long time. But that was in another time and another world."

"Well, she never mentioned any of that to me and we be first cousins too 'cause my father and her mother were brother and sister." By now Harold seemed to have drifted off into a world of his own, seemingly not noticing his pain or the dreadfully rocky tracks that the ambulance had to traverse.

Once back at the Clearing Station, Sam made it his personal responsibility to see that Harold was carefully installed into one of the rough wooden cots. There were nurses and a few doctors flying about, attending to the most badly injured first. Catching the eye of one of the prettier nurses, Sam explained to her that Harold was a distant relation of his wife . He asked her to take care of Harold for him, saying he would be back later when his spell of duty ended.

True to his word, Sam came back that evening and sat by Harold's bedside. It was obvious that the young officer's condition had deteriorated.

Sam gently stroked Harold's hand and started to talk quietly to him about Taunton and about life in the past that they both would have shared there in Somerset. He talked about the cattle market on Saturday mornings, a social occasion for all the local farmers and their wives - a thronging hub of humanity, with the townsfolk mingling in as well. He talked about swimming in the River Tone, just up from 'French Weir', which had been a favourite spot for the young lads and girls to lark around in and have fun together. He talked to Harold about his family, his brother, three sisters and his parents.

Although Sam had not met the Taylors, Winifred had often talked about them and so he knew the story of Alice May Taylor and of her rescue of the young woman from the River Tone.

Harold seemed to rouse himself and to smile. Sam felt comforted that Harold had heard his words.

Harold's breathing became irregular and then, as Sam watched, Harold took one last quiet, peaceful breath. At that same moment Sam saw a mist-like, spiral leave Harold. It seemed to float across the room and pass through the wall of the building, and then was gone. It was a moment Sam was never to forget, and the only person he ever talked to about it was his dear wife Winifred, or Winnie as he called her.

Sometime later, on a Monday afternoon, Mr. and Mrs. Taylor received a cable conveying the tragic news that their son, Harold, had been wounded on 14th May 1917. He had been taken to a casualty clearing station but sadly died of his wounds three days later.

THE ROLL OF HONOUR

TAUNTON OFFICER DIES OF WOUNDS.

It is with regret that we record the death of Lieut. Harold Richard Taylor, the eldest son of Mr. and Mrs. Theo. Taylor, of Roslin Villa, Richmond-road, Taunton. The deceased officer, who was 27 years of age, was educated at Taunton School, and was articled to Messrs. W. J. Villar & Co., auctioneers, of Taunton. Whilst in Taunton he joined the West Somerset Yeomanry as a trooper, but when his business took him to Malmesbury he transferred to the Wilts Regiment. At the outbreak of war he was engaged in the Government Valuation Department, and was mobilised with his unit. About 15 months ago he was given a commission, and transferred to the Surrey Yeomanry, and attached to the 77th Machine Gun Company. At the commencement of the present year he went to Salonica, where he was wounded on the 14th inst., and succumbed to his wounds three days later. Mr. and Mrs. Taylor received a cable conveying the sad news of their son's death on Monday afternoon. Their second son, Lieut. Bernard Taylor, R.F.A., who was wounded in France some months ago, is now Adjutant of aircraft defences in Lancashire. The greatest sympathy is felt for Mr. and Mrs. Taylor in their sad loss.

LIEUT. TAYLOR.

Mr. and Mrs. Theo. Taylor desire to return thanks for the many kind messages of sympathy they have received, and which they are unable to acknowledge individually.

Harold was buried in the Sarigol Military Cemetery, Kriston, Greece.

The news filtered through to Winifred from the Taylors and, as well as grieving the loss of Harold, she also now feared more than ever, for the safety of Samuel.

Every day, Winifred cycled for hours over the Somerset Levels and up into the Quantocks. She found the physical activity stopped her from thinking too much. She had been told by Elizabeth Alice Taylor that there were more plaques relating to the Uttermares to be found on the walls of Langport Church.

Cycling along the straight, willow-lined drove on her bike she could see the church tower a few miles ahead, as the church was situated on top of a hill, with the town spread out on its slopes. At the bottom of the hill was the River Parrett and its once thriving medieval port - now disused.

She pushed her bike up the hill, leaned it against the ancient stone walls of the church and, thankfully, entered the cool, rather musty interior. There were the plaques, just as Elizabeth Alice had described.

Winifred, pen and notebook in hand, took down all the relevant information. Studying it when she returned home, she realised that all these names related to the 'posh' side of the family. They had married surgeons, lawyers and one had even become Deputy Lord Lieutenant of Somerset. It was a member of this side of the family who had bought and held the Lordship of the Manor of Hatch Beauchamp for a while.

Winifred wanted to know more about these people who, it would appear, lived different lives from those of her own line of the family which had been mainly farmers. She decided a further visit to Hatch Beauchamp Church was in order.

Another sunny day and another cycle ride across the Levels. Propping her bike up against the exterior stone wall of the graveyard, she entered via the wooden lychgate and spotted the same church warden, Paul Coates, whom she had met before on her first visit to England. He was digging a new grave. There would be many to be dug in this sad year of 1917. Paul straightened up and doffed his cap to Winifred.

"Do you remember me?" asked Winifred.

"Sure, I remember ye Ma'am." he said politely. "Have ye come looking fer yer family agen?"

"Well, yes. On my previous visit you told us about the last John on the list of names and how he didn't get on with his brother, William, and how they shared a servant and mistress or some such story. I think Mrs. Elizabeth Alice Taylor was rather shocked and I didn't hear the end of the tale," and she added, "whereas I, on the contrary, do love a juicy story!" and she laughed uproariously.

“Oh! So do I!” Paul twinkled “Let’s have a sit down in the cool and I will tell ye all I know.”

Sinking down onto a pew side-by-side, he commenced. “I heard from me Granfer that John Uttermare, born 1779 - ye see his plaque there,” and he pointed with an even more bent and arthritic finger than it had been when Winifred had visited before, “he had a younger brother, William, born 1784.”

“This William left all his wealth to his two children, Mary-Anne Gamlin and Edward Morrish, who were both born out of wedlock. They were raised at Wiltown Farm, Curry Rivel. Their respective mothers, Anne Gamlin and Elizabeth Morrish, lived therc too, as servants of William. Folk hereabouts did gossip about it but, for the most part, t’wer just accepted that t’wer how things wer.

“The children went to school in the village, and t’wer said that Edward’s fether had been a sailor and had died at sea and that Mary-Anne’s fether had died when she wer a babe. Some folks believed it, some didn’t. My Granfer - ee didn’t!

“They be both dead now, but I also know that Wiltown Farm where William and his two children lived with his two servants, have passed into possession of a family called Lang, who are local brewers. I heard that t’was Edward Morrish who left it to them in his will. He never had any children of his own as fer as I know. Tis all a bit of a puzzle if yer ask me.”

“Well, yes, it is,” replied Winifred. “I wonder how that farm and its lands passed into that particular family?”

“Ye had best go and talk to them. It will be William Henry Lang who lives there now.”

So, another day and another bicycle ride, this time to Wiltown Farm at Curry Rivel where William Henry Lang, a widower, now aged sixty-six, lived with his twenty-three-year-old daughter, Hilda Mary. He was very welcoming and more than happy to talk about his own family history.

He told Winifred that his parents had been childhood friends with Edward Morrish. His mother, Ellen, was especially close to Edward. However, just before she died, she had told him things about her childhood that neither she, nor her husband had ever spoken of previously.

"Would you like to hear the story that she told me about Edward Morrish and how we came to inherit his home and land?"

"Of course, I would!" replied Winifred, settling herself comfortably in a large Victorian armchair. "I'm all ears!"

"Well," continued William Lang, "this is what my mother Ellen told me about Edward Morrish, born 1833 died 1905, who turned out to be the last descendant in the direct male line of John Uttermare, born 1673, on the 'posh' side of the family."

"T'is often said," William Lang mused, "history repeats itself, and that is especially true in families. There were those two Uttermare brothers, more than two hundred years ago now it would be, one called John, the eldest, and the younger, Richard. Trouble was they were both educated differently, with John going to The King's School in Sherborne, which really was for the sons of the clergy and aristocrats, and Richard going to the Blue School, which was for poor and orphaned boys.

"The harvests were good the year John started at his school but, by the time Richard was to go, there had been a succession of bad winters resulting in near famine here on the Somerset Levels. Money for Richard's education was not to be had."

He paused and then went on, “So their separate schooling turned them into completely different characters, and the two never did get on. John married into a wealthy family, the Colliers, and his descendants became lawyers and wealthy land-owning farmers - although some were tenant farmers of just a few acres. On the other hand, Richard married a farmer’s daughter, and his descendants were solidly farmers, almost to a man.”

With a wry smile William Lang addressed Winifred. “Which brings me back to these other two Uttermare brothers: John, who was born in 1779, and William, his younger brother, born in 1784.”

“My mother told me that John was dark and stocky, t’is a trait of the Meads, many of whom married into the Uttermare family. He was a quiet, thoughtful lad and very content living at home at Wiltown Farm, Curry Rival with his parents. William, five years younger, had always been a tear-away, never sitting still for more than five minutes. He had a shock of blond hair and was tall and willowy and, when fully grown, cut a fine figure in the Georgian attire of the day.”

“However, his Uncle James, who held the title of ‘Lord of the Manor of Hatch Beauchamp’, didn’t think much of him. There is a story handed down about that.”

“Oh! I would love to hear it,” said Winifred. “All this family history is wonderful!” So William Lang continued with his monologue.

“The story goes that one day, Uncle James, who was unmarried and had no children, came to visit his relations at Wiltown Farm on his chestnut mare, Queenie. Uncle James lived at Hatch Green Lodge, Hatch Beauchamp, which is some eight miles distant.

“Uncle James hitched Queenie in the yard and, coming into the kitchen, announced to the assembled family, ‘That horse will be the death of me.

As soon as I put her to the canter, she attempts to buck me off - in fact she's had me on the ground twice on the way over here!'

"Hearing this, William sneaked out of the house, unhitched the horse, and sprang into the saddle. All that the family saw from the open kitchen window was William, streaking past heading for the paddock and yelling, 'Do you call this a buck?' as Queenie repeatedly tried to unseat him.

"William spurred Queenie on, yelling and whooping as he went, heading for the flat open moorland behind Wiltown Farm. William was totally confident that Queenie would jump the rhyne that bounded the paddock from the moor.

"However, the horse had other ideas and, instead of gathering herself to jump, she raised her hind quarters and tossed William skywards. He landed in the rhyne which, fortunately, was not too deep but just full of silty black mud. Queenie stood still looking at William for two seconds and then turned and slowly trotted back to the farm. William, now very muddy, made his way home to receive a strong reprimand from his parents and Uncle James.

"As William grew up, his reputation as a womanizer went before him. Uncle James must have born this in mind when he made his Will. He left his title of 'Lord of the Manor of Hatch Beauchamp' and much of his estate to John - as was to be expected since John was his eldest nephew and heir. He also made a few endowments to other nieces, nephews and cousins, but William never got a mention.

"Nevertheless, William carried on his merry way! He was good looking and knew it! He and John were educated at The King's School, Sherborne, so they were both literate, unlike many yeoman farmers of their time. In his middle age he was made a magistrate, so must have been considered a just man and a pillar of the community.

"After leaving school, the two sons worked alongside their father's labourers on the farm. They mixed with them socially at village barn dances and met with them on market days. But also, being yeoman farmers, they belonged to the so-called middle class so they were invited to balls and soirées at some of the local manor houses such as Pitney Manor, Hatch Court at Hatch Beauchamp, and Montacute House.

"William was not only good looking but had a charming, easy manner with everyone. He might have been 'Jack the Lad' but he was kind and generous too. The girls of the village fell for him and were quite happy to slope off with him whilst they were haymaking or working in the fields together."

William Lang broke off his monologue here and, looking a trifle abashed, he said to Winifred, "You see, there is something about those times all through the eighteenth century and even into the first quarter of the nineteenth century, that you are probably not aware of. I should tell you, because it explains what happens next," and he coloured slightly.

"No, no, do go on, I'm quite broad-minded. Don't forget I am from the United States of America, and we are so modern there!" and she laughed at her own observation.

William Lang sat up in his chair and, leaning earnestly towards Winifred, he said, "According to my mother, Ellen, this is how things were in the countryside back then in 1800. She explained to me that, as soon as a young couple were perceived to be 'courting', it was understood that their friendship would most likely be an intimate one. If the young woman found she was going to have a baby, it was also expected - by the families, friends, and neighbours of the couple - that they would be wed. It was almost an unwritten rule that everyone adhered to."

William paused and added, "I know for a fact, from having seen my parents' wedding certificate and my own birth certificate and from what my family have told me, that my mother, Ellen, and my father were living together at Bowdens Farm across the fields from here, before they were married. I was born there, and they were wed a little while later, and no one seemed to mind. It's hard to believe that now, isn't it?"

William Lang paused again, "But I'm digressing," he said. "My mother also told me that, amongst the upper-classes, things were quite different. The daughters of the gentry were expected to remain virgin, so that the men of wealth and land that they married, could be certain that their offspring were legitimate."

"So," continued William Lang, "you see, when William tumbled in the hay with one of the village girls and swore undying love and affection for her in his charming way, she would have thought that he was the man she would marry, and that she would become the wife of a prosperous farmer."

"On the other hand, when he was invited to the soirées and balls of the local minor aristocrats, the 'Papas' probably thought that, if all else failed, this pleasant, literate young yeoman farmer would do."

"However," he added, "quite early in the eighteen hundreds, William's father died and left Wiltown Farm and its land to William. His brother John now lived at Hatch Lodge in Hatch Beauchamp having inherited Uncle James's estate and title.

"William's mother, Ann, had always worked hard in the farmhouse, organizing the servants, giving daily menus to the cook, and supervising the running of the household. Now getting on in years, she had need of more help, and so hired a twenty-year-old village girl called Ann Gamlin. Ann had worked on her father's tenanted few acres and had also helped her mother at home. She was a strong, stout young woman. She was what might be called comely, with brown curly hair, rosy red cheeks and merry eyes.

“She soon settled into life on the farm. William, of course, soon noticed her and charmed her. He would stop and talk to her and compliment her on how well she helped the cook, and how he enjoyed the meals she had helped prepare for the family. She in turn was flattered by ‘the Master’s’ attention. He always treated her respectfully, although she had heard about his reputation elsewhere!

“William’s aging mother started to rely on Ann, giving her more and more responsibility and treating her like a daughter. Ann became housekeeper in all but name. Things continued like this for five years or so and then William’s mother died.

“Almost immediately, William felt able to ask Ann if she would like to now become his housekeeper. He suggested that she should move into the large bedroom that his parents had occupied, with its commodious four poster feather bed. William still used the small bedroom he had slept in as a boy. He also suggested that he would like to come to her bed now and again! What could she say? She was flattered.

“Not surprisingly, a year later, her daughter Mary-Ann was born. No-one in the house or in the village seemed to mind. These things happened here in the countryside. But Ann expected more, having been bought up to believe that, if a woman became pregnant whilst in a stable relationship, the man concerned would most certainly marry her.

“‘So, we shall be wed now then.’ she coyly observed to William when he came to admire the new-born baby. ‘We shall do no such thing,’ he replied. ‘It wouldn’t be right for a master to marry his servant, as much as I am fond of you Mary.’

“‘Well, in that case,’ she replied, ‘you will no longer come to my bed at nights.’

"William being a kind, if bigoted, soul agreed. He didn't want to lose Ann, who was a very good housekeeper, and anyway he could seek his desires and pleasures elsewhere!

"The child, Mary-Ann was known by her mother's surname, and she addressed William as 'Uncle'.

"Things continued at the farm with Mary as housekeeper and with housemaids coming and going. As Mary approached middle age a new housemaid was employed. Her name was Elizabeth Morrish. She was about thirty years old and came from near Bridgwater. No-one knew much about her. She professed to have worked as a housemaid in the past, and her references bore this out. She was flaxen-haired and blue-eyed with a curvaceous figure. There were rumours in the village that she had been married to a sailor, but she never admitted to this. In fact, she didn't talk about herself, or her past, at all. She just got on with her work and minded her own business.

"It wasn't long before William, now aged forty-six or thereabouts, and even more handsome than in his youth, started to pay attention to Elizabeth. She feigned not to be interested but, like Mary Gamlin before her, was secretly flattered, and she also believed that the unwritten social mores of the time would hold good.

"She really liked William. He was a kind and considerate 'master'. She had need of love, as she had indeed been married to a sailor who had gone off to sea and had never come back. She could only assume that he was dead, and she mourned him. She missed a man's embrace, and she often 'visited' William in his small room at night.

"At such times, Mary Gamlin in the next bedroom, in her lonely feather bed, would pull the thick eiderdown up over her head and stick her fingers in her ears.

“When Elizabeth gave birth to Edward Morrish in 1833, Mary was furious!”

William Lang sat back in his armchair and said, “So there you are. I haven’t talked so much in years!”

“Well thank you.” replied Winifred. “You’ve really made it come alive for me. I could almost have been there at Wiltown Farm with Mary Gamlin, Elizabeth Morrish and William Uttermare, but it’s probably a good thing that I wasn’t!” and she and William Lang both roared with laughter.

“Well - there’s more, shall I go on?”

“You bet!” answered Winifred in her slow Illinois American drawl.

Chapter 13 – Edward Morrish

Born 1833 died 1905
William Lang continued with the long story that his mother, Ellen, had told him all those years ago.

"For the first eight years of his life, Edward lived at Wiltown Farm, Curry Rivel with his Uncle William, his mother Elizabeth Morrish, and Anne Gamlin - at that time William's servant. Edward had known Anne all his life. Also living with them was Mary-Anne the twenty-year-old daughter of Anne Gamlin.

"One night there was a lot of crying and shouting and Edward was awakened and roughly pulled out of bed by Anne Gamlin. She instructed him to get dressed and then bundled him outside the house. The stocky, middle-aged woman led the old pony out of its stall, pushed Edward up onto its back, and then climbed up behind him too. They had an uncomfortable ride to his Uncle John's farm at Hatch Beauchamp. During the journey, Anne had been 'spitting tacks' and when Edward asked her why all this was happening to him, all she would say was, ''Tis not right what is going on in that house, 'tis no place for a child, and I'll say no more 'bout it.' To little Edward, only eight years old, it was all very confusing.

"Edward carried on living at Hatch Green Farm, Hatch Beauchamp, with his 'posh' Uncle John for quite a while and it appeared that Ann Gamlin was now his Uncle John's servant.

"Edward was still being educated at the same school in Curry Rivel. This meant that he needed to wake up early each morning so that he could be driven six miles to school in the pony and trap. Uncle John's groom would be there at the end of the school day to drive him home again.

“Many of the children at the school had to walk similar distances, and amongst some of them - especially the older boys - a feeling of animosity was building up against little Edward.

“‘Who do ye think ye be, being chauffer driven like that? We know who ye really be,’ they jeered at him, as he walked in through the school gates. Edward didn’t understand the taunts. He just felt the dislike coming his way, and he felt lonely and afraid.

“There were only about thirty children at the school and only two classes. There were two recreation yards: one for the younger boys and all the girls; and one for the older boys. The two yards were divided by a stone wall, and it was over this wall that the jeering was often directed at Edward.

“This bullying behavior had been going on for a long time now, but had got worse since he had been taken to live with Uncle John who had styled himself Lord of the Manor of Hatch Beauchamp. However, amongst his own classmates, who had known him since the beginning of their schooldays, he was popular, and they even felt sorry for him, for their parents had told them that his father had been in the Royal Navy and had died at sea. This was what Edward himself believed.

“On one particular morning, thirteen-year-old Ellen Dawbin, who was hanging about in the combined junior boys’ and the girls’ yard, saw Edward arrive. He looked sad and tired.

“‘What’s up Eddie?’ she demanded, and he told her the sorry tale of what had been going on. She was a kind girl and, when she got home, she told her mother - who was also a compassionate soul - about it.

“‘Well, I know his mother, Elizabeth Morrish, who works for Mr. William Uttermare, and I’m sure she’s not happy about her son being taken away from Wiltown Farm, but what can she do about it? She be just a servant.

The little lad can come and stay with us during the week on school nights,' she said, and then she added darkly 'until those two brothers resolve their differences!'

"Edward and Ellen became very close, like brother and sister, with Edward living during the week with the Dawbins. They would walk to and from school together along the muddy, willow-lined path, along which ran - as always on the Levels - a deep rhyne. Neither of the children could swim, but they knew of the dangers of the deep ditch, and they knew to keep well away from the edge.

"One summer's afternoon, they were walking home from school together when they heard a rowdy group of big boys coming up behind them. These lads started yelling out obscenities that they thought made them sound clever, and pushed themselves between Ellen and Edward.

"'Be ee yer boyfriend then? Ee be a bit young fer ye baint ee? Ye don't want to mix with the likes of 'im, 'ee be just a little bastard ye know!' and two of them pushed Ellen into some brambles. Then two others grabbed Edward, one holding him by both feet, and the other by both arms. They swung him high in the air, as though they were tossing a sack of potatoes up into a wagon, counting, 'One, two, three!' and they hurled him into the muddy rhyne.

"Edward landed flat on his back with a huge splash. His feet felt for the bottom of the ditch, and he managed to stand up with water coming up to his neck. He flailed about trying to scramble towards the bank. However, the boys had other ideas, and one of them climbed down the bank, grabbed Edward, threw him backwards and pushed his head under the water and kept it there.

"By now other children coming home along the path, had gathered round to see what was going on. Ellen had picked herself up out of the brambles and pushed herself to the front of the crowd. Fear gripped her heart as she witnessed what the bully boy was doing. She jumped up and down, tears streaming down her face, screaming, 'Leave 'im alone! Leave 'im go!' A boy who was in her class - who she now remembered used to write his name as Henry M Lang and who lived at Hambridge - was coming along the path. Seeing what was going on, he immediately jumped down the bank and charged into the bully boy, sending him flying into the centre of the rhyne. Feeling beneath the water, he pulled up the seemingly lifeless body of Edward.

"'Help us get 'im up!' he shouted to Ellen and the other children. Once on the grassy bank, Henry, who was a well-built thirteen-year-old, and son of the local brewer, rolled Edward onto his side. Then he furiously pummeled Edward's ribcage and yelled madly at the limp body 'Breathe lad, breathe!' Ellen felt as though time had stopped. What would they tell Edward's mother if he died?

"Then Edward's body jerked violently and he vomited onto the grass. Henry took off his own coat and covered Edward. Ellen and some of the other children did the same. All the culprits had long gone.

"'You stay 'ere Ellen and keep 'im warm and I'll go and fetch his mother. She be at Wiltown Farm. 'Tis not far and we'll bring blankets and take 'im home when he 'av recovered a bit'

"Elizabeth Morrish duly arrived and did indeed take him home - back to his first home - Wiltown Farm where he remained for the rest of his childhood and until he was an old man. He lived there, as before, with his 'Uncle' William, his mother Elizabeth Morrish and his half-sister Mary-Ann Gamlin.

"As for Anne Gamlin who had removed Edward from Wiltown Farm and taken him to live with his Uncle John, she only rarely visited.

"In 1851, when Edward was eighteen, it came time for the census forms to be filled in. William Uttermare called Edward and Mary-Ann to him and declared that he had acknowledged them as his children, and that they would one day inherit his wealth.

"In earlier censuses he had referred to them as family servants or as visitors! In fact, all his wealth came down to Edward who had no children of his own. He, in turn, left it all to the Lang family to whom he felt very close, and to whom he felt he owed a debt of gratitude.

"The three young people, Henry Lang, Ellen Dawbin, and Edward Morrish grew up together and, in 1852, Henry married Ellen at Moorlinch Parish Church which was where her family now lived.

"As newlyweds they went to live at Bowdens Farm and Edward Morrish, who had been their Best Man, was their immediate neighbour, as he, of course, lived at Wiltown Farm, whose land was adjacent to theirs."

Coming to the end of his story, William Lang took a deep breath, and then continued, "Edward was very good to me all my life, and once told me that he was going to leave everything to me in his will. At the time, it seemed odd to me that he should have told me this but, after the conversation with my mother, Ellen, I better understood things."

William paused and seemed to drift off, remembering the past and then he went on. "As soon as Edward had passed away in 1905, I contacted his solicitor, fearing that there might understandably be challenges to the will from the Uttermare family. The solicitor told me that I was free to move into Wiltown Farm which was now empty. Edward had moved to 'The Elms' Curry Rivel some years before his death, with just a house maid and a cook to look after him."

"After his half-sister, Mary-Anne, died, Edward must have found Wiltown Farm too big to manage on his own," William continued. "I farm the land and have been carrying on the family brewing business. The solicitor tells me it may be many years before Edward Morrish's estate is settled, as he feels the will may be contested by existing members of the Uttermare family."

"And," interjected Winifred, "who are they?"

"Well," replied William Henry, "the only one left now that I know of is Thomas Mead Uttermare who used to live at Bowdens Farm just along from here, at Hambridge."

"I remember my father and I visited him there in 1908," replied Winifred, "and I met Elizabeth Alice Taylor and her three adorable children too. We all went together to Hatch Beauchamp Church to look at Uttermare plaques, and that's what set me off on this hunt."

William chuckled, "Thomas is living at Churley Farm now, over at Stoke St Gregory, so maybe that's your next port of call."

"Maybe I will pay him a visit," mused Winifred.

Chapter 14 – Thomas Mead Uttermare

The Last Uttermare - Born 1869 died 1949

For the second time in her life, Winifred wrote a letter to Thomas Mead Uttermare asking him if she could pay him a visit. He promptly replied saying he would be delighted to meet her again and that, if it was convenient to her, she was welcome to come to lunch the following Sunday after Chapel.

By return of post, she accepted his invitation and, a couple of days later, set off early after breakfast to cycle from Isle Abbots to the village of Stoke St Gregory.

It was a warm, sunny day as she rode along the country lanes. She noticed the masses of primroses on the grassy banks and listened delightedly to the birdsong in the willow branches above her head. All of nature seemed to be waking up and breathing a sigh of relief that winter was finally over.

She knew she was indeed privileged to be enjoying this moment on this morning of 1917 when so many young men from the surrounding villages were falling in battle. Her heart had been broken by Harold's death, but the warm sun on her face and the beauty of the countryside lifted her spirits and made her feel more hopeful than she had been for a while. She also felt intuitively that Samuel, her husband, would come home to her, safe and sound. Everyone thought of him as such a solid and reliable chap! He was bound to make it back!

Winifred arrived just before midday at a tidy, stone-built, thatched farmhouse. It had a garden at the front where daffodils were nodding their heads in the light breeze, adding to Winifred's feeling of well-being as she propped her bike against the garden wall. She marched confidently up the path. Using the well-polished, brass, knocker, shaped like a horseshoe, she knocked briskly on the front door.

It was opened by a young woman, dressed fashionably in a slim-fitting, cream-coloured, linen dress, with pearl buttons at the cuffs, which she had teamed with smart low-heeled, cream, leather shoes.

"Do come in, it's so lovely to meet you. We've all been so excited about your visit since Uncle Tom got your letter last week." The young woman introduced herself. "I'm Eunice Maud, Uncle Tom's niece. Come this way and meet everyone."

Winifred followed her into the beamed sitting room, and Thomas Mead Uttermare heaved himself up out of a large wing-backed armchair and, smiling, he came towards her. He clasped both her hands in his own gnarled ones.

"Welcome Lass, 'tis good to see ye agen. Ye don't know my cousin 'ere do ye?" and he indicated a youngish woman who introduced herself.

"I be Lilia Mead and you are very welcome. These two here are my children, although I can hardly call them that can I, they have grown so big! This is James and this is Fred." Two boys, James, aged fifteen, and Fred, aged twelve, shyly shook Winifred's hand.

Over lunch, which was local roast lamb followed by apple crumble and Somerset clotted cream, family news and history were exchanged. Winifred learnt that Thomas had come to live at Churley Farm just a couple of years earlier, after Lilia's husband Frederic had suddenly died too young at the age of forty-eight. She had been left with the farm to run and three young children to bring up. Eunice the eldest, was still only fifteen at the time.

Thomas was ready to leave Bowdens Farm at Curry Rivel. He said he rattled around that big place like a pea in a pod with only his housekeeper, Lois Hooper, for company. He had been more than happy to make the move.

Eunice proudly told Winifred that she worked as a solicitor's clerk in Taunton, getting the train there and back each day from the small halt on the railway line on the outskirts of the village. Winifred was much impressed, acknowledging and approving of, the increased independence that women were gaining - even out here in the depths of the English countryside.

The time sped by and, looking up from the meal table, Winifred noticed the sun dropping lower in the afternoon sky.

"I must be off," she sighed. "I have had such a wonderful time. Thank you so much, all of you!"

"You must come again soon," they all chorused from the doorway as she reclaimed her bicycle and peddled off, waving cheerily as she went.

Winifred's husband Samuel Tapp did come back from the Great War. He and Winifred went to live at Lydeard St Lawrence, near Taunton. They never had any children, but folk who knew them said they both seemed perfectly happy in each other's company, enjoying the quiet pleasures of gardening, painting, reading and taking part in village life.

Samuel died in Taunton on 14th January 1938 aged sixty-three and Winifred died a year later, on 31st March 1939 aged fifty-five - passing away peacefully in the village she loved, and back in the county of Somerset from whence came all her Uttermare ancestors.

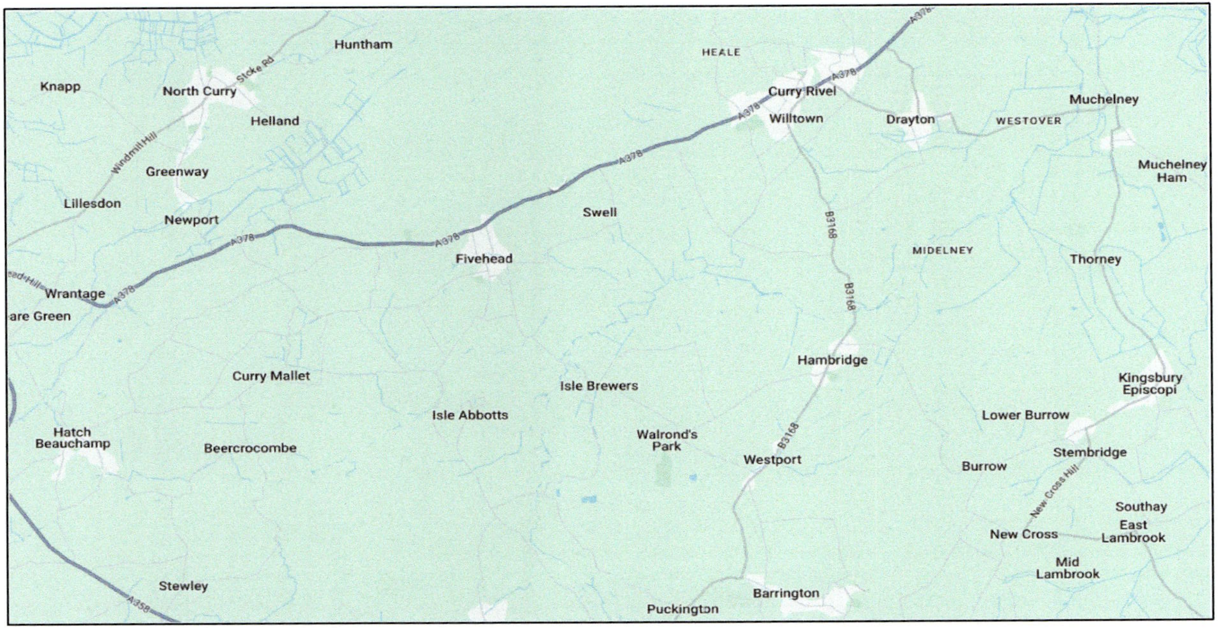

Map showing locations relevant to the story *(Google Maps)*

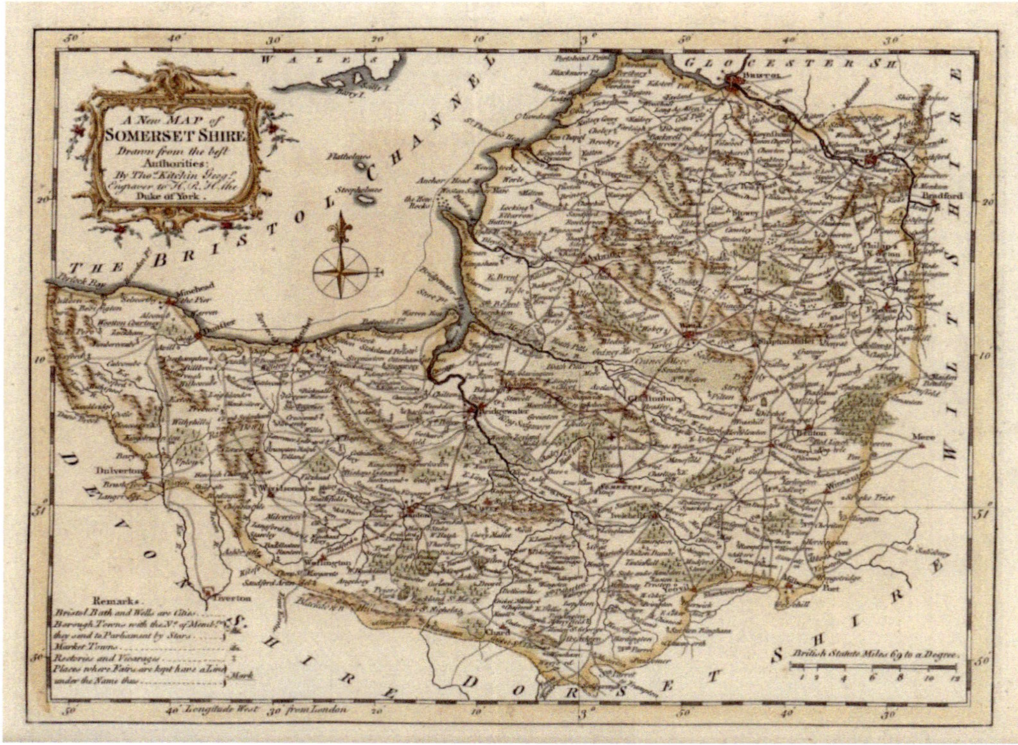

'A New Map of Somersetshire' drawn by Thomas Kitchin circa 1763
(copper plate engraving with hand colouring)

Epilogue – Claire and Ross

July 2022

Claire and Ross were once more back spending time in their one-hundred-and-fifty-year-old Catalan Farmhouse, or Mas as it was known, under the mountains of the French Pyrenees. Life, they thought, was beginning to return to something like normal after the intervention into the world of a tiny virus that had caused havoc in so many lives. Thanks to modern and brilliant science, the majority of the Western World was now protected by vaccines.

Then, hard on its heels, came another totally unexpected shock to the West. Russia had invaded Ukraine and huge destruction had been wrought. Millions of women and children had fled their homeland and who knew what was coming next?

Looking at the Uttermare Family Tree, now hanging proudly in its frame on the wall, Claire stood deep in thought and then voiced her musings to Ross.

"You know, all these people lived their lives, sometimes with earth-shattering events going on around them. They would have been affected in various ways, large and small, but I am not aware that any of them changed the course of history or played any major role that anyone remembers. They were not prime ministers, kings or queens, famous scientists, painters, musicians or reformists. Their names will not go down in history or be remembered - except by me!

"As the Bard said:

> 'All the world's a stage,
> And all the men and women merely players;
> They have their exits and their entrances;
> And one man in his time plays many parts,
> His acts being seven ages.'"

“And” she continued, “it’s the same for us. You and I have lived through some momentous events - even during the time that I have been doing this Uttermare project.”

Then, looking a little wistful, she quietly asked herself, “But who will remember me?”

“I will.” said Ross. “And so will our children, grandchildren and great grandchildren, all of whom will be added to your Family Tree.”

“You are such a sweet man!” chuckled Claire, and then she turned and, looking at each other, they both spontaneously burst out into gales of unrestrained laughter and inexplicable joy.

19th August 2023

The End

Disclaimer

Images in this book which are older than one hundred years plus the artist's life are no longer subject to copyright law and are in the public domain.

Family members who are currently living have given permission for the inclusion of the family photographs included in this book.

Place names and key historical events are based on fact. The names of people no longer living, found in this book, are all real and do not require permission for their use. Names of living people found in the book have either been changed or permission has been given for their use.

Acknowledgements

My grateful thanks to Jo Davies for editing and arranging publication of this book. Without her help it may never have seen the light of day.

To Liz Windett and David Taylor, newly discovered second cousins and fellow researchers of the Uttermare family tree, for their encouragement, enthusiasm and friendship.

To Henry Lang who generously gave me the Uttermare wills.

To my children and grandchildren for their constant love, and to Joss who always supports me in everything I do, including the writing of this book.

Sue Delves-Broughton
November 2024